Welcome!

Welcome to a year of holidays with Nick Williams and Carter Jones!

This is the first volume in a series of compiled short stories, all of which are centered around specific holidays.

Each story is a vignette that stands on its own and takes place from the 1920s to 2008.

When we read along, we get a chance to visit a place and a time which no longer exist. We get to see things as they might have appeared through the eyes of our narrator (or narrators).

Most of all, we get to discover where Nick and Carter are in the progression of their lives on that particular holiday in that particular year.

Included Stories

New Year's Day, 1979

Martin Luther King, Jr., Day, 1986

St. Valentine's Day, 1951

Washington's Birthday, 1948

Mardi Gras, 1975

St. David's Day, 1848

A Year of Holidays with Nick & Carter

Volume 1

Nick Williams Mysteries

The Unexpected Heiress

The Amorous Attorney

The Sartorial Senator

The Laconic Lumberjack

The Perplexed Pumpkin

The Savage Son

The Mangled Mobster

The Iniquitous Investigator

The Voluptuous Vixen

The Timid Traitor

The Sodden Sailor

The Excluded Exile

The Paradoxical Parent

The Pitiful Player

The Childish Churl

The Rotten Rancher

A Happy Holiday

The Adroit Alien

The Leaping Lord
The Constant Caprese
The Shameless Sodomite
The Harried Husband
The Stymied Star
The Roving Refugee
The Perfidious Parolee
The Derelict Dad
The Shifting Scion
The Beloved Bach
The Redemptive Rifleman
The Agitated Actress
The Manic Mechanic
The Loveless Lawyer

The Adventures of Nick & Carter

The Crooked Colonel
The Crying Cowboy
The Rowdy Renegade

Nick & Carter Stories

An Enchanted Beginning
Bells Are Ringing

Golden Gate Love Stories

The One He Waited For
Their Own Hidden Island
Chasing Eddie

Daytona Beach Stories

The Sailor Who Washed Ashore
The Lawyer Who Leapt
The Cuban Who Paid Dearly
The Demoiselle Who Departed

The Romantical Adventures of Whit & Eddie

Getting To Know You

'S Wonderful

You're The Top

In The Still Of The Night

Let's Misbehave

3/17/2020
Sean—
Let's get this party started!
John

A Year of Holidays

with

Nick & Carter

Volume 1

By Frank W. Butterfield

Published With Delight

By The Author

MMXX

A Year of Holidays with Nick & Carter, Volume 1

Copyright © 2020 by Frank W. Butterfield.

All rights reserved.

ISBN: 979-8-61-994862-2

First publication: March 2020

No part of this book shall be reproduced, stored in a retrieval system, or transmitted by any means–electronic, mechanical, photocopying, recording, or otherwise–without written permission from the publisher.

Brief excerpts for the purpose of review are permitted.

This book contains explicit language
and suggestive situations.

This is a work of fiction that refers to historical figures, locales, and events, along with many completely fictional ones. The primary characters are utterly fictional and do not resemble anyone that I have ever met or known of.

Be the first to know about new releases:

frankwbutterfield.com

YOH01-B-202000301

Contents

Compilation Preface..1

New Year's Day, 1979..3

    Preface..5

    The Story...7

Martin Luther King, Jr., Day, 1986......................41

    Preface..45

    Chapter 1..47

    Chapter 2..57

    Chapter 3..69

St. Valentine's Day, 1951...................................83

    Chapter 1..85

    Chapter 2..89

    Chapter 3..95

Chapter 4..101

Chapter 5..107

Chapter 6..119

Chapter 7..125

Chapter 8..139

Chapter 9..145

Washington's Birthday, 1948............................153

Preface..155

The Story..157

Note..175

Mardi Gras, 1975..177

Chapter 1..179

Chapter 2..193

Chapter 3..209

St. David's Day, 1848......................................221

Preface..223

The Story..225

Author's Note..243

About Frank W. Butterfield............................245

Credits...247

More Information...249

Compilation Preface

Welcome to a year of holidays with Nick Williams and Carter Jones!

This is the first volume in a series of compiled short stories, all of which are centered around specific holidays. Each story is a vignette that stands on its own and takes place from the 1920s to 2008.

When we read along, we get a chance to visit a place and a time which no longer exist. We get to see things as they might have appeared through the eyes of our narrator (or narrators). Most of all, we get to discover where Nick and Carter are in the progression of their lives on that particular holiday in that particular year.

. . .

Many thanks to the beta readers who helped me with these stories.

Very special thanks to Edward Lane for his patronage of this book!

New Year's Day 1979

Preface

The Hopkins Dallas is based on the Loews Anatole which opened at the same time. That hotel, known as the Hilton Anatole as of this writing, was built by Trammel Crow, developers of the Dallas Market Center and much of the surrounding neighborhood on either side of Stemmons Freeway (I-35E).

Enjoy!

The Story

Hopkins Dallas Hotel
2201 North Stemmons Freeway
Dallas, TX 75207
January 1, 1979
12:01 a.m.

It was a cold, icy night and Carter and I were dancing like we did when we were young.

The DJ had found an old version of Guy Lombardo and His Royal Canadians performing "Auld Lang Syne."

I closed my eyes as we moved around the dance floor, my left hand in his right and his other arm around my waist, holding me close, with mine around the small of his back.

We were celebrating the new year north of the equator for the first time in a long while. Normally, we went somewhere warm for the holidays, but that year, we decided to stay in San Francisco. It was the first time in more than ten years that we'd done so.

And the weather in Dallas had welcomed us with cold, frigid hands. As we were dancing, it was about 25 outside and the mercury was steadily dropping. Trees and power lines all over town were coated with ice thanks to the fact that it had been sleeting earlier that day. On TV, we'd heard how power was out in different parts of the city. Fortunately, the hotel had never lost power and had been able to take in a few guests who needed a warm place to spend New Year's Eve.

Our plane had arrived at Love Field on the previous afternoon, when it was a bit warmer. We'd been driven over to the hotel, which wasn't too far away.

We'd been greeted at the front door by Charles Marcus, the general manager. He'd previously worked for another hotel in the area. I wasn't sure which.

Charles had contacted me in the middle of November and invited us to spend New Year's Eve in Dallas. He was pulling together an invitation-only party which would be exclusively gay and held inside the private club at the top of the hotel called The Fourteenth Floor. He said he was selling tickets for a hundred dollars a pop and how all of the money raised would go to our foundation.

Since that was the case, we couldn't resist. I promised I would personally match whatever he raised and multiply his take by ten. If he could sell a hundred tickets for ten grand, I'd add another ninety and make it an even hundred. Easy enough.

When we'd arrived, he'd showed me his records. He'd sold just shy of five hundred tickets and to folks from as far away as Phoenix and Baton Rouge.

I'd congratulated him on a job well-done and written a check to him, personally, so that the total came to an even five hundred grand and he could pay out the whole amount to the foundation in one lump sum.

After Carter and I were up in our suite, I'd realized that might have been a mistake for tax reasons and otherwise...

. . .

Once Guy Lombardo had finished singing, the DJ started up a disco version of the same song.

Carter let go of me and then began to do his usual boogie. It involved him swiveling his hips and grinding them up and down while doing a two-step dance move with his big feet that he'd picked up when we used to spend the holidays in Rio. When he got down on the dance floor like that, a small pack of admirers would always gather.

At 58, he was still the most handsome man on six continents (I'd checked).

And he looked like he could have been in his 40s. His reddish blond hair was only partially streaked with white. His muscles were just as big as they'd ever been. And, at 6'4", he still commanded most every room he walked into, even though there were plenty of kids, anymore, who were his height or taller.

We were both wearing the 1978 version of a white tie tux. Our outfits matched, even down to the bow ties, button-up vests, and white patent leather pumps. The only thing we were missing were top hats, but I had stopped wearing a hat back in the early 70s and had no desire to do so again.

His trousers were skin-tight and made of some kind of stretchy polyester. I didn't like how it smelled. Neither did he, but he'd decided the look was what counted. He'd practically bathed in British Sterling cologne, his new favorite scent, to cover up the chemical stench.

Cologne was a new thing for him. I didn't mind it. His sense of smell was much stronger than mine, so, if he could stand it, so could I. But I preferred a whiff of something simple, like Aqua Velva, when I kissed him.

My trousers didn't have the same awful odor, since they were made of wool and had a smooth silk lining, like they were supposed to. And I didn't wear cologne, either. I just splashed on after-shave and that was all I needed.

In any event, Carter was doing his moves and an admiring crowd was beginning to gather, like always happened. I stood where he'd left me and watched as he got down and grooved to the disco beat.

Whenever we went out to the discos, anymore, I always let him do his thing and enjoy being admired by the crowd. For myself, I preferred to find a nice spot where I could watch everyone as they moved and chatted with friends and attempted to hook up (and sometimes succeeded). I looked around to see if I could find any such thing.

After a moment or two, I spied the DJ's booth, which was elevated above the dance floor and across the room from where I was standing. Through thick glass that reminded me of a bank in a rough part of town, I could see the black kid who was manning the turntables. He had on a pair of big headphones and was smiling and nodding to the beat as he made a motion with his hand that made me think he was putting the needle on the next record.

Sure enough, the disco version of "Auld Lang Syne" faded away. I then heard a familiar count to two followed by the crowd cheering as "Le Freak" started up.

Most everyone who'd been standing on or sitting by the edges of the dance floor (single guys, by the look of things) made their way to dance to the song that had been popular for a while and didn't seem to be losing any steam.

Carter's admirers pushed him towards the middle of the dance floor. From what I could see, he appeared to be having fun. So did they. I smiled in admiration, happy to be watching and not part of the action.

With the crowd moving onto the floor, I took the opportunity to make a wide circle around the room in an attempt to find refuge in the DJ's booth. I was hoping that, since I was the owner of the joint, he might let me sit on a stool or something and watch the night away from a lofty distance.

...

On my way around, I decided to make a stop at one of the bars and pick up a rum and Coke.

"Mr. Williams!" exclaimed an enthusiastic redhead who had to be about 25, if that.

I smiled. "How's business?"

"Considering everyone shoulda stayed home in this weather, I'm doin' fantastic." He eyed my outfit and, with a grin, said, "Classy threads!"

"Thanks."

Giving me a professionally seductive smile, he asked, "What can I get you?"

"Dark rum and Coke on the rocks."

"Captain Morgan?"

I shook my head. "You should have a bottle of Gosling's. It's a requirement for every Hopkins bar."

He grinned. "We do. And we were wondering why we had it on hand. Every other place I've ever worked only had Captain Morgan. Is it your favorite?"

I nodded.

He laughed. "Gosling's and Coke. Coming right up." He turned and headed towards the middle of the bar.

He was wearing the same thing all the other bartenders were wearing: a tight black t-shirt with our logo ("Hopkins Hotels") just above his left nipple. On the back was a silk-screened image of the Mark Hopkins on Nob Hill in San Francisco in silhouette. Under that, it read, "Welcome to '79" in the same style as our logo. It was a special thing Charles had ordered just for the night.

Carter had mentioned how the silhouette should have been of the Dallas hotel. He had a point. With the three buildings (of varying heights) clustered as they were in a triangle along with their distinctive pyramid roofs, they presented an impressive outline from the freeway as we drove in from the airport. They were supposed to grab your attention and, apparently, they did.

According to Charles, the local papers had complained about them being too unique when the buildings were finally finished. More than one person had admitted to police that they were gawking at the hotel when they'd hit the car in front of them during rush-hour traffic.

One of the other bartenders walked by right then. A blond with a tight crew-cut and an earring in his right ear, he appeared to be in a bit of a rush. And he looked frazzled. In fact, he was in more of a rush and more frazzled than was normal for even a New Year's Eve. To be honest, he looked panicked.

I watched as he disappeared through a pair of swinging doors. Something told me to follow him, so I left a hundred-dollar bill on the bar and did just that.

. . .

Behind the swinging doors, I found the kitchen. No one was cooking but there were two kids washing glasses. They were loading up trays with dirty glasses and lining them up to go down a kind of assembly line on rollers and through an automatic dishwasher.

I stopped by a big stainless steel table and looked around. The two kids were the only ones I could see.

Walking over to them, I tapped on the shoulder of the one closest and asked, "Did you see a bartender come charging through here?"

The kid, who looked like he might have been Chicano, frowned at me and asked, "Eh?"

I looked at the other one, who might have also been Chicano. They were both attractive and were filling out their black t-shirts and Levi's (the other part of the uniform) quite handsomely. Both were about 5'5" with black hair, also cut short like everyone on staff whom I'd met.

The second one frowned at me a little as he said, "You can't be back here, mister." He had a slight accent.

I grinned. "Sure, I can. I own the place."

His black eyes opened wide. "Oh, Mr. Williams. So sorry."

"No problem," I said. "Did you see a bartender run through here?"

Shaking his head, he said, "The only person I saw here was Mr. Marcus. About five minutes ago, I think."

That set off an alarm bell, but I had no idea why. "Where'd he go?"

With a sudsy finger, he pointed to a doorway. "There. To the elevator, I think."

I smiled at them both and said, "Thanks."

I heard, "Sure thing, Mr. Williams," as I jogged to the doorway and rounded the corner, trying not to slip on the floor in my brand-new shoes.

. . .

The bartender I'd followed was, just then, stepping into the service elevator about twenty feet away.

I waved at him and said, "Hey!"

As soon as he saw me, he began to vigorously stab a button on the panel to his right. I thought I saw a big plastic bag of something white, maybe coke, in his left hand, but I couldn't tell.

I was about halfway to the elevator when the doors closed. Under my breath, I muttered, "Damn."

Looking around, I noticed there was a darkened office to my left. I thought I heard a sound coming from somewhere inside, so I walked over to investigate.

A desk with a small stack of boxes stacked on top was pushed against a wall and just under a window that looked into an office beyond where I was standing. I looked around for a light switch and found it. I flipped it on, but nothing happened.

I heard the sound again. Since I was closer, I realized it was a moan. And it was coming from inside the inner office.

The entire time I'd been in the kitchen area (all two or three minutes), I could hear the music coming from The Fourteenth Floor where Carter was doubtlessly grinning at the guys who were trying to boogie with him.

I felt sorry for them, sorta, since they were all going to be disappointed.

He liked to dance. And he liked to be admired. But he would gently rebuff any attempt made by anyone to make any sort of move on him. And he was a big guy, so few guys did, which was a good thing. For them.

The music began to change. As I walked into the inner office to find out who was moaning, I could hear a tune which assured me that Chaka Khan would soon be telling us how she was every woman.

The room was dark. It took a moment for my eyes to adjust. The only piece of furniture was an empty desk. On the surface, I saw two lines of white powder, shining brightly in the dim light. Next to them was, unsurprisingly, a razor blade.

I licked my finger, touched one of the lines to grab a few granules, and then put it on the tip of my tongue. As soon as I did, it went numb and the numbness spread quickly. It was primo coke.

Over in the corner, I saw a body on the floor and on its side and facing the wall.

I walked over and knelt down. I put my hand on the shoulder of whoever it was and gently turned them in my direction. It was Charles Marcus. And he was bleeding, but not much, from a gash above his forehead.

"Charles?"

He moaned.

"Hold on. I'll get you some help."

I heard him whisper, "Nick."

"Yeah?"

"Nick."

"I'm right here."

He grunted. "No, no."

"What?"

"Nick Reynolds."

I got it. "Is that who attacked you? Nick Reynolds?"

"Yes..." He moaned again.

. . .

"What's your name?" I was talking to the second dishwasher.

"Juan." He looked at my hand and frowned.

I glanced down. There was blood on my fingers.

"You OK?" he asked.

15

"Yeah. But Mr. Marcus is in that office by the elevator. Someone slugged him. Do we have a First Aid kit around here?"

Juan nodded as the first dishwasher looked at me, his mouth agape.

"It's dark in there. See if you two can carry him in here and"—I turned to point at the stainless steel table—"put him here. Find some towels and then see if you can clean his wound. Do you think you can do that?"

Juan nodded wordlessly.

"I'm going to go find a doctor, if there's one here."

"What happened?"

"Do you know who Nick Reynolds is?"

Juan nodded. "He's a bartender."

"Blond?"

"Yes."

"I think he slugged Mr. Marcus. Go get him and see if you can get him cleaned up. OK?"

Juan nodded. "OK."

. . .

I quickly found the red-headed bartender just about the time Melba Moore started singing "You Stepped Into My Life."

"Hey there, Mr. Williams!" he said with a big smile. We were standing at the end of the bar where I'd been earlier. He pointed to a glass. "I got your drink right here." He was talking a mile a minute and managing to do so over the thumping sound of the music. "Looks like it's melted, which is no surprise, since it's so hot in here." He pulled on his shirt which had significant wet spots under his arms. "I can pour you another one if you want."

"Skip it," I said, more curtly than I meant to.

The quick shift in his expression let me know he'd just heard his boss talking. He was suddenly serious. "Everything OK?"

"I need a doctor."

He stepped back a little. "A doctor?"

"There's been an accident in the back." I had no desire to spill all the beans.

"Oh," he said, nodding thoughtfully. He then turned and looked out over the dance floor. After a moment, he snapped his fingers and pointed. "I see Dr. Joe."

I chuckled. "Dr. Joe? "

"He's some kind of fancy doctor in University Park. Super rich."

"Can you go get him?"

"Sure," said the kid as he bounded around the end of the bar.

I grabbed him by his sweaty arm and hissed, "Quietly. Don't make a fuss."

He nodded, his eyes wide with curiosity, and said, "Sure."

. . .

Pulling a dark blue handkerchief (the same color as his skin-tight t-shirt) from the left back pocket of his painted-on button-up Levi's, the man wiped off his face with a big smile. He then stuffed the hanky back where he'd found it, making sure to leave the top part sticking out. He held out his hand. "I'm Joe. I understand you need a doctor?"

I shook. "Nick Williams."

His grip was firm. He was about 6'4" or so, trim, had salt-and-pepper hair (cut as short as everyone else's), and a mustache. If we'd been at home, the kids would have called him a "Castro clone." Or, more likely, just "Daddy." He was probably my age, if not older, and def-

17

initely handsome with a wide smile and a generous mouth.

"Yeah," I replied. "He's in the back. Follow me."

"Sure."

I walked around the bar and he followed.

As I was about to go through the double doors, he asked, "Aren't you hot in that tux?"

I shook my head. "Nope. But, then again, I haven't been dancing."

. . .

"How're you feeling?" asked the doctor as he leaned over his patient who was stretched out on the stainless steel table.

Charles sighed. "A little woozy." His head was propped up by a small stack of towels. His white shirt and black tux were dotted and streaked with dried blood. He was a mess in a handsome sort of way.

"What happened?"

"I was socked in the face."

Dr. Joe nodded. "That explains the black eye..."

"Yeah." Charles seemed to be reluctant to talk about whatever it was that happened. I wondered about that.

I said, "You must have hit your forehead on the desk,"

"That would explain the cut," said Dr. Joe. "I'm impressed that you're still conscious."

"Well, I did see stars," said Charles with a wan smile. "Like in the cartoons."

Dr. Joe grinned as he used a towel soaked in rubbing alcohol to clean up the wound on Charles's forehead. "I've never been knocked out, but you're not the first one to tell me..." His voice faded.

"What?" I asked. Juan, Manuel (the first dishwasher), and I were hovering and watching Dr. Joe do his thing.

"We really need to get him to a hospital. He's going to need stitches." He thought for a moment. "Parkland isn't that far away."

Juan said, "It's too slick outside."

I added, "Besides, on TV tonight, they were saying how all the hospitals are packed with people who've slipped on the ice or were in wrecks."

Dr. Joe nodded, looked at me, and frowned. He then dabbed a little bit more on the wound and said, "I'm going to take a closer look, Charles. This is going to hurt."

The other man nodded.

Juan picked up a clean towel from a stack he'd put on the table for the doctor to use. He rolled it up tightly and then said, "I will put this in your mouth. You can bite down."

Dr. Joe said, "Good thinking."

Charles opened his mouth and Juan gently placed the rolled-up towel inside.

"Bite down," said the doctor.

Charles did just that.

Leaning down, Dr. Joe used his towel to poke and prod at the wound.

Charles made a moaning sound and kicked his left leg.

The doctor then stood erect and patted Charles on the shoulder. "Sorry about that."

"Mmm," was the reply.

"I can do the stitches myself." He looked at me. "I'll need a small needle and some thread." He glanced over at the open First Aid kit. "I have everything else I need in here."

"Mmm, mmm," said Charles.

Juan said, "Open up."

Charles did that and Juan removed the towel. After working his jaw a little, Charles said, "There is a big box of sewing kits down in the housekeeping office. It's on Mark's desk."

"Who's Mark?" asked Dr. Joe.

"He's the head housekeeper."

"You've got a *man* running that department?"

Cutting in, I looked at Juan. "Do you think Manuel could find those sewing kits?"

Nodding, he replied, "Oh, sure. I send him right now." He took his buddy by the arm, talking to him in Spanish, and walked him over to the doorway that led to the elevator.

Once they were gone, I said, "Charles? Tell me what happened."

He glanced at the doctor, who was rummaging through the First Aid kit.

"Spill," I said.

"Well, you're gonna fire me. I spent all the money I was going to give to your foundation. I was hoping I could double it." He looked miserable. I felt sorry for the guy. I didn't care about the money. There was lots more where that came from.

"First things, first," I said, snapping my fingers impatiently.

"Nick Reynolds is the one who slugged me."

"Why?"

"Because he found me snorting a line of coke."

"So?"

"I had my stash sitting right there. I couldn't resist."

"So he knocked you out, grabbed the stash, and then got in the elevator before I could grab him."

"I guess."

"How much did you have?" asked Dr. Joe.

I held up my hand. "Hold on." I looked at the doctor. "No cops."

He frowned. "Cops? What cops? Who's going to come out tonight, of all nights, anyway?"

"Then why'd you ask?"

He sighed. "Because Big Tony is here tonight. He's the local dealer to all the money gays. I saw him sitting over by the windows with a couple of bodyguards. This is just the kind of thing he would pull."

I looked down at Charles, who was as white as a sheet. "How much?"

"Two kilos, minus three lines."

"Jesus," whispered Dr. Joe. "That's gotta be close to half a million bucks!"

I shook my head and crossed my arms. "Where'd you get it?"

"Big Tony, just like he said."

I looked at the doc. "And who's Big Tony?"

Dr. Joe chuckled. "He's the last person you would imagine. He's—"

Juan burst into the kitchen. "Boss!"

"What?"

"Come quick." He motioned towards the elevator.

I ran around the table, trying not to slide in my shoes, and followed him.

. . .

Manuel was standing next to the elevator door, holding it open, and looking at the unseeing eyes of its sole occupant.

Nick Reynolds, the blond kid who'd stolen a shitload of coke, had been murdered. He was curled up in a fetal position, his head turned towards the car's ceiling in an unnatural way. If his eyes hadn't been open, it would have looked like he was sleeping. But he wasn't.

Reaching inside, I pulled out the STOP button on the panel. Looking at Manuel, I said, "It's OK. You can let go."

Behind me, Juan said something in Spanish.

Manuel let go and stepped back.

I knelt down and took a good look at the body. That was when I saw the marks around the kid's neck. He'd been strangled with something thin. I pushed his head back. Based on the angle of the bright red line, it appeared that someone taller than him had done the job.

I stood and looked at Juan, who was watching me with interest. "Is there a walk-in icebox up here?"

He nodded and turned around. Pointing to a door on the right, just past the two offices, he said, "There."

I walked over and opened the door. The room was empty, but the refrigeration was on. It was cold. There were no shelves or furnishings of any kind, however. It was empty.

I closed the door and walked into the kitchen and over to where Dr. Joe was bent over, looking at Charles's scalp, and quietly talking to him. "I think this might only need four or five. It shouldn't hurt too much."

"Doc?"

He glanced at me. "Did you get a needle and thread?"

I shook my head. "Nope, but I've got a corpse."

"Nick Reynolds?" asked Charles, quietly.

"Yeah. Someone strangled him. He's in the elevator."

Dr. Joe straightened up. "Damn."

I nodded. "We have an empty walk-in where we can keep the body. But I want you to have a look, first."

"What about me?" whined Charles.

Dr. Joe patted his shoulder. "I'll be right back." He looked at me. "I need that needle and thread."

I nodded. "I'll go get it myself."

. . .

After Juan and Manuel moved the body into the walk-in, I got in the elevator and took it down to the basement. Once the door opened, I found myself at the end of a hallway. The smells and sounds let me know I was near the kitchen, which was still open and would be all night.

Even though I owned the joint, I'd never been "back of house," as they called it in the biz, so I had no idea where housekeeping was and I'd forgotten to ask Juan.

Wandering around, I eventually found myself in the lobby, across from the front desk. I walked across the marble floor, suddenly realizing that the music being played up in The Fourteenth Floor was coming through the lobby speakers and competing with the waterfall in the middle of the atrium. The two cute kids behind the desk were acting out the letters from "Y.M.C.A." like human semaphores and giggling as they did.

I walked up and said, "You two should be on stage."

One of them—tall, lanky, and with long brown hair—looked at me and grinned. "To be honest, Mr. Williams, we're both hoping to go to Hollywood."

The other one—a blond, thin, and on the short side—blushed and straightened his tie and vest. "Sorry, Mr. Williams. We're just clowning around."

"It's fine. Do you have a sewing kit down here?"

The blond nodded and then knelt down to open a cabinet behind the desk. He reached for something, stood, and handed it over. "Will this do?"

I opened the small gold box and found two needles, a small pair of scissors, three kinds of thread, and a couple of buttons, all neatly packed inside. "Perfect." I reached into my wallet and pulled out two hundred-dollar bills. "Happy New Year."

. . .

"Here you go." That was me handing over the sewing kit to Dr. Joe.

Charles was sitting up on the stainless steel table, looking slightly less miserable than he had earlier.

Juan and Manuel were back at the dishwasher, dealing with a whole new load of dirty glasses that must have been brought in by the barbacks while I was gone.

Dr. Joe inspected the box and then nodded. "This'll work fine." He grinned. "Now I need a couple of shots of vodka."

"Disinfectant?" I asked.

"No, I can use the rubbing alcohol for that. I need the shots for Charles, here."

. . .

"How's everything going, Mr. Williams?" That was the red-headed bartender. Al Green was singing his cover of "To Sir, With Love." The dance floor was empty except for guys in leather slow dancing together. Carter was nowhere to be seen, but I had bigger fish to fry.

"Fine. I need a bottle of vodka."

He paused for a moment as two guys wearing matching rainbow suspenders and red t-shirts walked up. "Uh, sure. Any particular brand?"

"Any Stoli?"

He grinned. "Sure, we got one bottle. You want that?"

I nodded.

He walked away and, as he did, one of the guys next to me said, "I know you're from San Francisco and everything"—he had a thick Texas accent—"but no one I know around here drinks communist vodka, comrade." He wobbled a little as he talked.

"Hey!" said his buddy. "He's a fuckin' billionaire. He ain't no commie!" The two were obviously soused.

"I don't give a good goddam whether he's a fuckin' Rockefeller, Bobby! I don't like Russian anything!"

"Oh, yeah?" asked Bobby. "My grandmother was Russian." He grabbed his plainly visible endowment under his button-fly Levi's. "You like this, doncha? Enough to squeal for it. It's a quarter Russian."

The first guy dropped to his knees and began to fumble around with the buttons of Bobby's jeans.

I tapped him on the shoulder. "Save that for later."

He angled his neck around and glared up at me. "Ain't none of your business, comrade."

"Keeping a liquor license *is* my business." I hooked my thumb over my shoulder. "Take it back to your room."

Bobby tousled his friend's hair. "Come on, you know I don't like you to do that in public."

"That's not what you said at the Round-Up the other night."

"I was drunk."

His friend started fumbling with the buttons again. "You're drunk now."

I was about to say something again when a bartender I hadn't seen before suddenly appeared. He was about Carter's height and build and had black hair that was, unsurprisingly, cut short. "Hey, you two. Take it to your room." The bartender had a deep voice that cut right through the opening rhythms of "Instant Replay."

The guy on his knees looked up. "Who's gonna make me?"

The bartender took two steps and reached down. He grabbed the guy by the back of the shirt and stood him up in one quick move. "I guess I am." Looking at me, he asked, "What should I do with him, Mr. Williams?"

"Put his tab on my account if he agrees to stay and keep everything where it should be, all nice and legal.

If he doesn't, throw him out into the icy cold of night." I tried not to grin. I knew that, if Carter had heard me, he would have scolded me for my high-hat talk.

"Hear that, fella? You can drink for free or you can hit the road. Your choice." He still had the guy by the back of his shirt.

"Come on, Rick," said Bobby. "Don't make a scene."

"Fine."

The bartender let go and then patted Rick on the shoulder. "What'll it be?"

"Gin and tonic. *British* gin."

"Me too," chimed in Bobby.

Tilting his head towards the other end of the bar, the bartender said, "Come down here with me, y'all, and I'll get you set up." He winked at me as he positioned himself between the two guys and escorted them away.

I turned to see the bottle of Stoli sitting on the bar, but no red-headed bartender.

. . .

"Commie vodka?" That was Charles.

Dr. Joe looked at me. "And a whole bottle? I just want to help him ease the pain, not black out."

I walked over to where the clean glasses were stacking up and grabbed one. Back over at the table, I unscrewed the bottle, poured a finger of vodka, and then handed the glass to Charles. "A potato is a potato, no matter where it comes from."

Dr. Joe laughed as Charles and knocked the drink back in one gulp.

"Damn," he said with a wince as he handed the glass back to me.

I noticed Dr. Joe had everything he needed to do the job all laid out on a towel. I asked, "Do you need any help? I was a corpsman during the war."

He shook his head. "No, but thanks. This won't take long."

I nodded and then realized there was something I'd completely forgotten about. I looked at Charles and said, "I'm sorry, but I am gonna have to fire you. We can figure out something else for you to do, though, if you want."

He sighed. "I understand."

"I'm going to go see if there are any gay cops out there. But I'm not going to mention the coke."

"You should probably get rid of the two lines I didn't do, then."

Juan turned around from where he was stacking glasses and grinned guiltily. "Oh, Manuel and I took care of that."

I shook my head with a slight frown but didn't say anything. If I fired everyone who did a line of coke at work, I would probably lose about half my employees. Maybe not that many, but it would be a significant number.

It was just a fact of life. I didn't like it, but that was how things had been for the past few years.

Dealing the stuff, however, was a big problem. If the cops found out a deal had happened on the premises, that would be a bigger problem. If they found out my general manager had been involved, we might lose our liquor license, or worse.

. . .

"Yes, sir, Mr. Williams!" That was the red-headed bartender.

"Do you know if there are any cops here, tonight?"

He frowned. "Do you mind if I ask what's going on?"

I nodded. "I do mind. I can tell you all about it later, but, right now, I'm hoping you might know whether there's a gay cop out there on the dance floor."

He shrugged and then looked over. After a couple of moments, he grinned. "Sure. I see two, in fact. One works vice for Dallas P.D., bless his heart, and the other is a homicide detective in Plano. Either of them do?"

"Is the one from Dallas a sergeant or higher?"

"I think he's a sergeant. He does undercover work on the prostitution side of things. Downtown. Women only." From the look on the kid's face, I couldn't tell if he liked the guy or not.

"Do you know him?"

"I've blown him in the backseat of the car he was using during an undercover sting. It was kinda hot, except..." He held up his left pinkie and waved it around in the air. "But he's got a nice apartment at Mockingbird and Greenville near SMU and I've been to a couple of parties there. He seems to be a magnet for guys from frat row who like to experiment."

"Can you go get him?"

. . .

I held out my hand. "I'm Nick Williams and I own the place."

The man shook and smiled. It was dazzling. He also had a gap tooth. I could see why anyone, male or female, would go for him. He was about 5'8", had short blond hair (but not too short), and was wearing a mustard yellow t-shirt and Levi's (zip-up, not button-fly). His forearms were veiny and covered in thick chestnut hair. "Nice to meet you, Mr. Williams. What can I do you for?"

"I understand you're a sergeant for the Dallas PD. Is that true?"

He nodded. A wariness entered his bright blue eyes.

"What's your name?"

"Albert Keller."

"We've got a problem."

He crossed his arms. "We do?"

"One of my employees has been murdered. He was strangled with something thin and dumped in the service elevator. I have reason to believe he was carrying a couple of kilos of coke on him and that was why he was murdered."

Sergeant Keller nodded and pressed his lips together while I talked. He asked, "Do you have the coke?"

I shook my head. "I think he was carrying it when he was murdered."

"And how do you know his body was dumped in the elevator?"

"I don't. I saw him going down. About five minutes later, two of my other employees found him inside the car."

"How do you know they didn't do it?"

"They're too short. The scar on his neck indicates whoever did it was a few inches taller."

He made a face. "You know we really should call homicide, right?"

"But when will they get here?"

"Good point." He took a deep breath. "OK. Where's the body?"

...

Kneeling down, he turned the neck left and then right and then nodded. "You're right. The assailant was definitely taller." He stood and rubbed his hands together. "How tall would you say the victim is?"

I shrugged. "About my height. 5'10"."

He made a circle motion with his finger. "Turn around."

I did just that.

"Oh, damn. I need a chair. Let's go back into the kitchen."

. . .

I felt a slight tug as Sergeant Keller pulled on the thread he'd strung around my neck. "I think that's about the right angle." He was literally breathing down my neck. The stench of booze was pretty strong. "Joe? How tall would you say I am?"

Dr. Joe looked over at the two of us. He was done with the stitches and was pouring a second shot of vodka for Charles, who'd been complaining about the pain. "Maybe 6'5", but it doesn't matter. I know who did it."

"You do?" asked the sergeant as he leaned against my shoulder and got down off the chair he'd been standing on. "Why didn't you say so?"

"You were having so much fun playing homicide. I didn't want to spoil your fun." He was smiling, but I could hear bitterness in his voice.

"Fuck you, Joe," said the sergeant as he swaggered over to the doc. "Gimme a swig of that."

"Drinking on the job, again, Albie?"

The sergeant shoved the doctor who only smiled at the attempt. "I told you never to use that name again!"

"Guys!" That was me.

Dr. Joe looked over at me and winked. "Lovers' quarrel."

"I ain't your lover and I never was," retorted the sergeant as he tried to grab the bottle from Dr. Joe's hand. He couldn't, though, since the doc was several inches taller and was holding it above his head with a smarmy grin on his face.

"No, sir. You're cut off."

"Fuck you, Joe."

"Little guys like you can't hold your liquor."

"Cut it out, you two," I said as I walked over and grabbed the bottle from the doctor. "This is getting us nowhere." Before the sergeant could take the bottle, I turned it upside down in a sink and shoved the top into the drain. Turning around, I crossed my arms. "Doc, you said you know who did it."

Dr. Joe shrugged. "Sure. So does your ex-GM. And Juan and Manuel. And Keller. We all know who did it."

"Who?" I asked, exasperated.

"Tiny Watson."

I rolled my eyes. "OK. Lemme guess. Tiny is seven feet tall and Big Tony is, what, five feet even?"

Dr. Joe grinned. "Big Tony is 4'10" and Tiny is 6'5"."

"And they're lovers," added Juan as he was loading up trays of clean glasses onto a cart.

"Great," I said. "Are they out there dancing?"

The sergeant shook his head. "They're out there, alright, but Big Tony doesn't dance. He's holding court in that big corner booth over by the windows that have the great view of downtown. He and Tiny and that other bodyguard of his, Big Jim Mendoza."

"I suppose Big Jim is five foot even."

"No," grinned Dr. Joe. "He's tall *and* big. About 6'3" and probably 290 or 300. He used to be a linebacker for the Giants."

I looked at the sergeant. "So, we know who did it. What do we do?"

Crossing his hairy arms, he thought for a moment. "We can't confront him. Too many people and there's no way to get backup right now."

"What if we just wait until morning?" asked Dr. Joe.

I shook my head. "I heard on TV that it's only going to be getting colder. We need to find a way to deal with him so that—" I suddenly realized there was no good outcome. If he was arrested, then the drug deal would become news. We could lose our liquor license. We'd just opened the hotel and we were about to go down in flames. I was probably over-reacting, but—

Sergeant Keller interrupted my thinking. "You're worried about what'll happen when news gets out about all this, right?"

I nodded. "I can't imagine we'll be able to keep our license. I don't care about that for myself. If this place closes, I'd hardly notice." I shrugged. "In fact, I could sell it and probably turn a profit. I just don't want any of the guys out there to have to find another job in this economy. It's not fair to them."

Dr. Joe said, "It's not the job, Mr. Williams. It's the fact that they know they can be openly gay and that you'll protect them. That's a big deal, what with Anita Bryant and everything she's doing these days."

Sighing, Keller nodded. "He's right about that. And you're probably right about your license. The TABC—that's the Alcoholic Beverage Commission—they're cracking down on places known to tolerate drug use."

Dr. Joe snorted. "If they were really serious, they'd have to close down every restaurant and bar in Texas."

I asked, "So, what do I do?" I was drawing a blank.

The sergeant thought for a moment. "Well, you do have more money than Jesus, right?"

I chuckled. "Sure."

He scratched his nose and then sidled up to Dr. Joe and put his arm around the man's waist. "What if you paid Big Tony and his team to get out of town?"

"And go where?" I asked as Dr. Joe kissed the sergeant on the top of his head.

"Lemme think."

Right then, we all heard the DJ say, "Since they've decided to grace Dallas with their presence, I thought I'd remind our two hosts of what they're missing by being here."

"What's that mean?" asked Dr. Joe.

I shrugged.

Then I heard the song and grinned as the doctor and the sergeant laughed.

Dr. Joe sang along with Peter Allen. "*I go to Rio...*"

"*...de Janeiro...*" added Sergeant Keller as we all laughed again, even Juan and Manuel.

. . .

"I hear you have a proposition for me. That so?" That was Big Tony. He was standing in between Tiny and Big Jim. The three of them made an interesting trio. For such a short guy, whose head was at the height of the other men's elbows, Big Tony had a big voice.

"I do." I was sitting on the side of the desk in the inner office where I'd found Charles on the floor earlier. Sergeant Keller and Dr. Joe were standing behind me. I was having a hard time not swinging my leg in time to the beat. The DJ was playing one of my favorite songs, "H.A.P.P.Y. Radio" by Edwin Starr. I really wanted to get up and dance, but I needed to take care of Big Tony and his buddies, so I sat still and gave them my stone face.

It had taken me about twenty minutes to come up with a plan and get everything ready, including a quick trip to the front desk. Once I was set, we'd sent Juan out with a message that I had a business proposal for Big

Tony and that I wanted to see all three of them in my office.

They'd come right in, which was no surprise. Keller had told me that Big Tony was a small-time hood. His racket was selling all manner of party drugs to the Dallas gay community which was surprisingly big. But it was small potatoes compared to what else was out there. Two kilos of coke would have been a big sale for him.

I figured that was why he'd likely paid Nick Reynolds to steal back the stash from Charles. Big Tony was probably hoping to sell the same two kilos two or three times. If he did it right, all the cops would end up with was a dead faggot or two who no one would have spent too much time investigating, particularly if there was no family to make a fuss.

Keller had said that usually there wasn't. Most of the guys in Dallas had come from small towns in Texas, Louisiana, or Oklahoma. They'd probably been disowned by their families or were, at least, pretending to be living a swinging bachelor's life in the Big D with promises to eventually settle down and get married to some gal back home.

For Big Tony, it was a good racket, if he could keep it up. The cops wouldn't care. One less fag was fine by them. But Keller didn't say that. He didn't have to.

Once they made their way back to the office, Keller had insisted on frisking them. They, of course, had balked. After threatening to call in more cops, they'd finally agreed. To no one's surprise, Keller had found the wire used to strangle Nick Reynolds, but not the coke.

I said, "One of your guys killed one of my employee's"—I held up the piano wire Keller had found in Tiny's coat pocket—"and stole back the two kilos of coke you sold to my GM."

Big Tony shrugged. "So?"

"You don't deny it?"

"No."

I looked at the wire and then at Tiny. "What were you thinking of? *The Godfather*?"

The man's sullen expression didn't change.

"What's your proposition?" asked Big Tony as I stuffed the piano wire in my pocket.

"How'd you like to relocate your operation to somewhere warmer?"

He frowned. "Where?"

"Rio."

Big Jim, who'd been scowling down at me, shuffled his feet at that and almost smiled. But not quite.

"Why Rio?" asked Big Tony.

"More room to grow your business."

He looked me up and down. "That takes money."

I nodded. "I know."

"I hear you're loaded."

"I am but I'm not an idiot. I can't be blackmailed, and I don't throw my money into the wind."

He grinned at that. "That sounds like something out of a movie, right there."

"Maybe so," I admitted, trying to remember if it was or not.

"How much?"

"Ten million."

He looked at me for a long moment. "How do I know this is on the level?"

I moved my leg, the one that was falling asleep, and said, "You don't. But I can make you a promise. If you're not out of my hotel by sunrise, I *will* call the cops *and* the feds, since I doubt you're paying any taxes, which you should, by the way, and have you arrested."

Big Tony grinned. "And have the TABC come down on you for being a known drug spot? I don't think so."

"I can build ten more hotels here in Dallas and serve everyone apple juice and hardly see a blip on my bottom line." I crossed my arms. "So you can hang around and wait for the ice to melt and for the cops to come or you can leave now with fifty grand in your pocket. You head down to Mexico City and wait there and you'll get the first million. Then, if you go to Rio, you'll get another million a month until you've got the whole ten. But if I find out you're back in the country, the deal is off, and the feds will get a call. I'm sure the IRS would be very interested to find out how much you've been paying in taxes the last couple of years. You go to Brazil and stay in Brazil and your worries are over. No murder rap, no federal indictments, just warm sand and all the *cachaça* you can drink."

"What the hell is that?"

Big Jim said, "It's like Brazilian tequila, boss."

Tiny said, "This is the offer of a lifetime, hon."

I reached into my tuxedo jacket and pulled out an envelope. "Here's the fifty grand to add to the briefcase of cash that Charles Marcus gave you earlier. And there are instructions about what to do along the way to let me know you're keeping your part of the bargain." I tossed the envelope over to Tiny who deftly caught it. "Now get the hell out of my hotel and out of this country and enjoy your new life."

I stood up, pushed past Tiny, and, breathing slowly and deliberately, made my way into the short hallway and opened the walk-in door.

I knelt down next to Nick Reynolds and put my hand on his cheek. "Sorry about all this, kid. If you have any family, I'll make sure we take care of them and they'll never be the wiser." I pulled the piano wire from my coat pocket and placed it on the cold concrete floor next to the kid's body for the cops to find whenever they arrived.

The next part of the plan was for Charles to call the cops after Big Tony and the others were gone. He would claim to have found the body and then, in his rush to get help, he would say he slipped and hit his head on the floor. When asked, I would say that I had found him and then brought in Dr. Joe and Sergeant Keller. Juan and Manuel would back us up.

Once the dust was finally settled, Charles would announce he was quitting. I would find somewhere else for him to work. But I'd made him promise to stop dealing and that, if he did again, I'd turn him over to the cops. It was a kind of mutual self-destruction blackmail pact.

When we were going over everything, I'd offered Juan and Manuel a big cash bonus for their help. They'd gratefully accepted.

Keller had turned me down, saying he didn't want to add bribing a cop to the list of offenses we were all collectively committing.

Dr. Joe had accepted a couple of weeks in Hawaii, on me, provided the sergeant went with him as his guest. The sergeant had grinned and kissed Dr. Joe right then. Things were looking hopeful on that front, which was good.

I patted Nick Reynolds on the cheek again and said, "Goodnight, sweet prince." I was sure that line was from a movie or a book, but I had no idea which one it might be. Carter would know, however.

I stood and walked out of the walk-in. I saw the elevator door close as Tiny waved at me and Big Jim winked while Big Tony scowled with his arms crossed.

As I walked into the kitchen, I found Charles sitting on the table and making out with Juan while Manuel was pressing himself against Juan's ass and grinding in a suggestive manner.

It was a pretty picture, I had to admit. Charles was handsome, in a roguish kinda way, with his stitches and slightly bloody black tux. Juan and Manuel were just plain hot, all tightly packed into their t-shirts and jeans like they were.

Too bad I didn't have a Kodak on me.

. . .

As Sylvester sang "Mighty Real," I made my way across the dance floor. Carter was in the center. In the last hour or so, he'd lost his jacket, his vest, his bowtie, and his shirt. His chest was glistening under white and golden red hair. With one hand up in the air, he was gyrating in a circle and showing his off his muscles to a cheering circle of fans.

As Sylvester's oohing began to fade, I recognized the less frantic beat of Olivia Newton-John singing "A Little More Love."

His fans began to pair off for some slow dancing.

Carter's gyrating shifted gears and, spying me in the distance, he pointed and then crooked his finger, calling me towards him.

I had no choice but to head his way. I was a fish on his hook. He was reeling me in.

Once I was standing in front of him, looking up and grinning at how handsome he was and remembering, for the millionth time, how much I loved him, he slowly pulled off my coat. He tossed it out into the crowd. Someone caught it. I didn't see who since I was staring into his shining emerald green eyes.

He undid my bowtie and, after stripping it off my neck, he slowly and seductively stuffed it down the front of his trousers. It was a move that was utterly ridiculous and charming and sexy in the most unexpected way.

Still moving to the music, and without saying a word, he began to unbutton my vest. I expected him to take it off, but he didn't. He left it on me, flying loose.

Next, he pulled my shirt out of my trousers and then began to unbutton it all the way down. Each button was held in place with a diamond-topped gold stud, a gift from him a couple of years earlier.

He tossed each one out to the crowd.

And each one was caught by someone who, if they didn't pawn it or sell it, would have a story to tell their lovers and their friends.

By the third one, the crowd began to cheer whenever the person caught it. There were six in all.

Once he had me undressed the way he wanted, he pulled me in close and wrapped his big, sweaty arms around my body.

We danced like we used to when we would listen to Jo Stafford on the hi-fi, with my head on his shoulder, doing a slow shuffle in a circle.

With perfect timing, the DJ began to mix in the song Carter and I had been dancing to anytime we had the chance to do so over the past few months. It was Olivia singing "Hopelessly Devoted to You" from *Grease*.

It was a magical moment, to be in his arms and next to him and more in love than I could ever remember.

He leaned down, kissed me deeply and passionately, and I began to see stars.

Pulling back, he asked, "What've you been up to, Boss?"

"Nothing in particular, Chief."

He grinned. "There's a couple of drops of blood on your right shoe, Nick. Tell me all about it later."

I laughed. "I will."

Martin Luther King, Jr., Day
1986

"In those days, everything we ever did always ended up being about AIDS. Who was dying? Who was dead? Which memorial service were we going to? I know the world around us kept going on, but, for me, at least, it pretty much stopped until maybe 1994 or so."

—Anonymous

"I try to remember that we fight as a ragged people to outlast the calamity so that others can sleep as safe as my friend and I, like a raft in the tempest."

—Paul Monette, *Borrowed Time: An AIDS Memoir*

Preface

The details I mention in this story about the parade are based on the front-page article entitled "Marchers honor Dr. King" from the final edition of the *San Francisco Examiner* dated January 20, 1986.

Chapter 1

1198 Sacramento Street
San Francisco, CA 94108
January 20, 1986
4:47 a.m. PST

I was sitting in the great room of our house on Sacramento when I heard a pair of size 14 feet pounding their way down the circular stairs and then cross the marble floor and heading in my direction. Looking up from my book, I asked, "What are you doing down here?"

With a yawn, Carter, my husband of going on 38 years, rubbed his head and said, "I woke up and you weren't in bed or in the bathroom, so I thought I'd check on you." By that time he had plopped down on the sofa next to me and put his arm around my shoulder. "Whatcha readin'?"

"One of your books."

"Oh? Which one?"

The Beginning of All My Tomorrows.

He snorted. "Jesus, Nick. That trash?"

I chuckled. "Is that any way to talk about one of your biggest bestsellers?"

He sighed, put his feet up on the coffee table, and sank down in the sofa little. "It's cold in here."

"Of course it's cold, fireman." Using the book, I pointed to the empty fireplace.

He sighed and then got up. "Now I get it." He walked over, knelt down next to the fireplace, and began to lay out logs in the hearth.

"Get what?"

"You were sitting there and sending me vibes to wake up so I could get a fire going down here because you were cold."

I chuckled. "No, I didn't."

He turned to look at me. "I distinctly heard you call my name. It's what woke me up."

I shrugged as he began to roll up sheets of newspaper. "I don't know what to tell you, fireman." Then I suddenly remembered something. "Well..."

"Uh, huh," said Carter in a very self-satisfied tone of voice.

"I was just reading the rape scene in the book."

"And?"

"And I was wondering why you would print something like that."

He pulled out one of the fireplace matches and lit it. After carefully setting fire to the newspaper rolls, he sat back on his haunches and said, "You know, no one knows how to set fires quite like a fireman."

"I know. In fact, I believe I was the one who first said that."

He nodded but didn't reply.

As I marveled, for about the ten thousandth time, at how handsome his broad back was, I said, "But what about that scene?"

"What about it?"

"You're being evasive."

He nodded without turning as the tinder all began to catch and start to spark a little. "You're right. I hate that scene."

"Lemme guess. Bulworth told you it's what sells." David Worth Bullington was Carter's right-hand man at WJ Publishing. Bulworth was a nickname he'd been given at Yale and it stuck. He was a pompous ass who, in the twelve years he'd been working for Carter, had turned WJ from a smaller imprint to the powerhouse it had become. The reason? He knew what would sell and what wouldn't.

"You got it."

I closed the book, leaned forward, and dropped it on the coffee table.

"Why are you reading it?" asked Carter.

"Ben asked me to." Ben White ran Monumental Pictures, a movie studio based in Culver City that I happened to own.

"Well, y'all better hurry. Columbia and Paramount are both in talks with Martina's agent." Martina M. Mitchell was the author of the book I'd just tossed on the coffee table. It was her fifth book since '78 when she'd been signed by Bulworth to publish under the WJ banner in the Talisman line of steamy romance novels.

"I told Ben I'd let him know today how I felt. When I read the rape scene, I suddenly understood why he asked me to look at it."

Carter stood and looked down at the fire which was building and beginning to put off some heat. He put his big hand on the mantel and said, "No movie is gonna be made with that scene in it."

"I hope the hell not."

He turned to look at me. Crossing his arms over his big bare chest, he crooked his head a little. "So why did I hear you call my name?"

"Probably because I was trying to figure out how I wanted to express my disapproval without sounding like a total ass."

He shook his head.

"What?"

"Where is the Nick who would just come right out and say it?"

I shifted a little on the sofa, suddenly feeling like he was putting me on the spot. "Maybe, at 63, I know better than to do that."

"Don't give me that bullcrap, Nick. I'm 65 and I think I'm getting even more opinionated than you ever were." He frowned a little. "What the hell would you say to old George Hearst? Hopefully you wouldn't just sit there and try to figure out what to say."

I shrugged again as the tears came. That had been happening a lot lately.

Carter was immediately at my side. He pulled me close. "Nick, I'm sorry."

"No, I'm sorry."

"Why are you up, anyway?"

"I was thinking about my meeting in DC."

He sighed. In a quiet voice, he said, "Of course."

I was suddenly angry. "Those assholes! People are dying and have been dying for years and we have all the money in the world, and they won't let us help!"

Carter pulled me in tighter. "Just think about our meeting in Paris next week."

I nodded. "I know."

In a soothing voice, he added, "Maybe this time—"

I pulled away from him. "We've been saying that to each other for too long." I crossed my arms as he frowned at me. "Maybe this time, they'll let us set up a clinic. Maybe this time, they'll take our money. Maybe this time—" I jumped up off the sofa. Looking down at him, I said, "We're out of time. Everyone is dying."

He pressed his lips together and then, in almost a whisper, said, "I know, son, I know." Suddenly, his green eyes were turning red. He looked, like he did more and more as he got older, like a lost little boy. Well, not so little at 6'4" and covered with muscles, but...

I got down on my knees and looked up at him. Putting me chin on his leg, I said, "I'm sorry, Carter. I shoulda kept my big mouth shut."

He rubbed his hand through my hair. "Well, at least you didn't hold back."

I gave him a wan smile. "I guess I didn't."

"How about we fly back to DC today and you take all that fire back to the Secretary's office and let him have it?"

"How about tomorrow? Today is the parade and we have a promise to keep."

He leaned over and kissed my forehead. "You're right. We do."

. . .

"Mr. Nick?"

I opened my eyes and looked over the back of the sofa to see Ferdinand, our gardener and ersatz chauffeur, standing there and looking down at me. He wasn't smiling but he wasn't frowning. That was his version of a happy face.

"Yeah?" I asked with a thickness in my voice.

"The breakfast is ready."

I realized I was sleeping on top of Carter, whose arms were holding me tight. With a smile, I said, "Good morning, sunshine."

The sides of his mouth lifted just a little. That was his version of a grin. "Good morning."

"Did Doris make it back from Salinas?" She'd been our cook for over twenty years. One of her many cousins lived in Salinas and was sick. Carter and I were sure it was AIDS, but Doris hadn't said anything about that. All she would say was that he was having trouble eating anything and was wasting away. We'd offered to have him moved to a hospice in Monterey, but he'd told Doris he wanted to stay at home. He was the only child of his parents, who were both dead, and was living in the house where he grew up.

"No. Gustav has cooked."

I heard Carter say, "I'm hungry, Nick. Get up."

Ferdinand winked at me and then headed back to the kitchen.

Instead of waiting for me to get up, Carter decided to take matters in his own hands or, rather, his own arms. Somehow, while holding onto me, he quickly stood up and put me down on the floor. At 65, he was as strong as he'd ever been.

I turned around, looked up at him, and said, "That was a neat trick, Chief."

He kissed my forehead. "I got a million of 'em."

. . .

Breakfast was a baked egg dish which was... interesting. Doris was one hell of a cook and anything that either Gustav or I could make would pale in comparison. But this was something... well... different.

Carter, who was picking at his food, asked, "New recipe, Gustav?"

"Yes," he replied, beaming, as Ferdinand wolfed down his food. "I find in magazine. *Sunset*."

"What's that spice?" I asked, managing to swallow a bit.

"Marjoram. I find fresh on Mission."

Carter and I both nodded. The marjoram was the only thing I could taste. In moderation, it would have been good...

"No bacon?" I asked.

"There is chicken."

I wanted to ask, "Who the hell has boiled chicken baked into eggs for breakfast?" but didn't. Instead, I carefully said, "This is certainly *unique*."

Gustav, not really catching my meaning, continued to beam as he took a bite of his toast. "Yes. I think so."

Ferdinand, who was eating a lot faster than he normally did, handed his plate to his husband. "More."

Using the spatula, Gustav dished out a healthy portion and said something in Czech.

Ferdinand took his plate, grunted, and dug right in.

While Carter and I watched him eat, the phone rang. We both said, "I'll get it."

But I was closer and beat him to the phone on the wall. "Yeah?"

"Nick?"

"Doris? How are you?"

She sniffed. "I'm... well... I'm..."

"Did something happen?"

"*Luis* just died."

I took a deep breath. "I'm so sorry. What can we do?"

"Nothing. I just called it in." She suddenly gasped with a sob.

"Is Maria there?" That was her girlfriend of almost ten years.

"Yes."

I heard a noise on the line. Then: "Nick?"

"Maria? Are you OK?"

"I'm just peachy. I told Doris to call you so you'd know it might be a few days before we make it back up to the City. Hold on." It sounded like she put her hand over the receiver. I heard her say, "Why don't you go out back, hon? I'll let Nick know all about it."

"OK," replied Doris.

I looked over at the table. Three pairs of eyes were looking at me under three furrowed brows. I nodded and mouthed, "He passed."

Right then, I heard Maria say, "Nick?"

"Yeah?"

"I didn't wanna say anything that Doris might hear, but I found Luis's will about a week ago and had already looked at it. I shouldn't have snooped but I did, so who the fuck cares, right?"

I chuckled. "Right. What does it say?"

"He left everything to Doris, including the house."

That wasn't surprising. Doris's mother had been his favorite aunt. Luis and Doris had been the only kids in their generation to grow up as only children. They'd practically been raised together even though they'd lived over a hundred miles apart.

"Anyway," continued Maria, "the will wasn't the only thing I found."

"Oh?"

"Luis took out a second mortgage on the house last summer. And he was behind in his payments. I went to the bank on Friday and made one of his payments, but—"

"Which bank?"

"Bank of America." I could already here the relief in her voice.

"Don't worry about a thing. I'll pay off the mortgage.

Both of them. And you're gonna need a lawyer. I'll call Kenneth here in a minute and he'll take of it all. All you two need to do is take care of yourselves." I dreaded asking the next question since I already knew the answer. "Will there be a funeral?"

"Of course the fuck not."

By that time, Carter was on his feet and standing next to me.

"Those bastard uncles will make sure no priest will bury him."

"What about cremation?" I asked.

"That's what he wanted." I heard her stifle a sob. "Um, Nick?"

"Yeah?"

"I can put up with a lotta shit, but I can't deal with *la familia*." That was how she referred to Doris's big, sprawling family.

Carter, who'd been listening in, grabbed the receiver. "Maria? It's Carter." He held out the phone so I could hear the other end.

"Hi. Did you hear all that?"

"I did. Like Nick said, don't worry about anything. You two just take care of what needs to be done there and come back home when you're ready. As for la familia"—his pronunciation was pretty awful-", *I'll* call Tico." That was Maria's oldest uncle who could be a real sumbitch. "Scratch that. Nick and I will go see him before we head out for the parade."

"Oh my God! Thank you, Carter."

I looked at Carter as I heard Maria begin to cry in earnest over the phone.

Chapter 2

Buy Better
2759 Mission Street
San Francisco, CA 94110
January 20, 1986
8:22 a.m. PST

Roberto Martinez (known as Tico to friends and family) owned a number of small grocery stores throughout the Bay Area and up and down the Central Valley. They catered to the Mexican-American community and were, in most cases, corner stores with a variety of names. If someone didn't know the store they were in was owned by Mr. Martinez, there was no way to otherwise tell that was the case. He didn't brand them as such.

The biggest of his stores was located on Mission, in the first block north of 24th Street. It went by the name of Buy Better and was usually festooned with white and yellow banners that advertised the current specials. That was where Mr. Martinez could be found seven days a week. He lived behind the store, in a modest apartment that dated back to the 40s, according to Doris. She'd never been invited inside.

Mr. Martinez was just a couple of years older than Carter but looked like he could be 80. On the couple of occasions when I'd met him, I had the impression he wanted people to think he was older than he was.

As usual, parking was difficult to find. Carter was driving. We were in his newest toy, an '85 Mercedes G which was nothing more than a box on wheels. A fancy box, being a Mercedes, of course. But Carter liked the head room.

And, although Carter hadn't said as much, we both knew that Mr. Martinez always loved to look at fancy cars. He would, of course, have already read about ours in the paper. Someone at the *Chronicle* had decided it would be entertaining to tell their readers about how we'd flown to West Germany to pick up the car and then flown it back with us in our Boeing 757 combi freighter jet. They'd failed to mention that we'd been using the jet to shuttle much-needed medical supplies from France and West Germany to Kinshasa, in Zaire, since there was nothing sexy about that.

In any event, we found a place to park on Capp Street, just south of 24th. It took about ten minutes to get to the store since we had to find our way around the crowd streaming onto the escalator and the stairs that went down to the BART station below 24th and Mission. It was a holiday. But not for everyone, obviously.

The store, of course, was buzzing with Monday-morning shoppers. Buy Better offered a five percent discount on Mondays before 10. They were famous for the discount and had a very loyal set of customers.

As we walked in, Carter said, "Let me handle this."

"Sure thing, Chief." I had no desire to deal with Mr. Martinez. He didn't like me one bit. He only barely tolerated Carter, to be honest.

"There's Isabel." That was Mr. Martinez's oldest daughter.

I looked around. "Where?"

"At the customer service desk."

I nodded. "I'll go talk to her while you deal with the old man."

Carter took a deep breath. "Wish me luck."

I patted him on the back. "Good luck."

. . .

"Nick!" A woman with big black hair who was wearing glasses dashed around the counter and pulled me into a big hug. She kissed me on the cheek and then pulled back to look at me. "What brings you to Mission Street?"

Isabel O'Malley was the oldest of all the cousins. According to Doris, her parents had both been 18 when she was born back in '34 or '35. Doris wasn't sure which. Isabel had married her high school sweetheart. She and Bobby O'Malley got married two weeks after graduation from Mission High in the summer of '52. The family had been shocked, but not that not shocked. Her Aunt Juana had married a guy with the last name of MacKenzie a few years earlier.

Like her aunt, Isabel never had any kids. After three years of wedded bliss (every member of the family agreed on that fact—something that was unusual in itself), Bobby had been driving home from his job down in Burlingame and had been rear-ended on El Camino by a truck whose driver didn't see the red light and plowed right over his Chevy. He lasted about two days at San Francisco General before he died.

Isabel had been devastated, of course, but had decided she was going to go to work for her father and had never looked back. She'd been over at the house for dinner a few times and had never once mentioned Bobby.

I knew we would see Isabel. She was at the store seven days a week, just like her old man. But on the drive over, I hadn't even thought about how I would break the news about Luis. From her happy expression, I could tell she didn't know.

I tried to figure out how to tell her but, before I could, she leaned forward a little as a big frown formed on her face. I must have waited one beat too long.

"What? Why are you here? What's happened? Is Doris OK?"

I swallowed and nodded. "Sure. She's fine."

Her eyes narrowed and then she put her hand over her mouth. "Oh my God! *Luis.*"

Tears suddenly sprang to my eyes as I nodded. I couldn't speak, so I kept nodding.

She pulled me in for another hug. "*Dios mío*, I can't believe it." She began to sway from side to side.

After a moment, she stepped back again and wiped her eyes with the sleeve of her brown sweater. "*Papi*? Is that where Carter is?"

I nodded again.

"Excuse me, Mrs. O'Malley?" An elderly woman was suddenly at my elbow.

Isabel sniffed and put on a brave smile. "Hello, Mrs. Hanahan. How are you?"

"I'm fine, dear. How are you?" The old woman, whose white hair was pulled back into a neat bun, looked puzzled and a little alarmed.

Isabel sniffed again and then laughed a little. "I'm just fine. These allergies are really bad this year, don't you think?"

"Oh, yes, my dear. Mrs. Prince, my upstairs neighbor, hasn't stopped sneezing since the new year."

"Goodness," replied Isabel as she slid around the counter. "The usual twenty?"

"Yes, please."

I stood and watched as the old woman slowly pulled her checkbook out of her straw purse and got to the business of writing a check.

As I watched her, I tried to figure out what Marnie (my stepsister and the best secretary a guy could ever have) would do if she was with me. I put my hand in my pocket and felt for one of the hundreds I kept there for just such moments. Keeping my eyes on Mrs. Hanahan's slow and precise handwriting, I pulled it out and let it drop to the floor.

"Two fives and ten ones?" asked Isabel.

The old woman cackled a little. "Hasn't changed in ten years, has it?"

"No, ma'am."

"I only wish Mr. Reagan would do something about my social security." She tore off the check and handed it over. Looking up at me, she said, "I hope you have something put away, young man."

I smiled. "A little. But I'm not a young man. I'm 63."

She waved me away. "Tell me what you think 63 sounds like when you're 95 like I am."

"Mrs. Hanahan," said Isabel, "this is—"

"You dropped something," I said in a rush. I was enjoying not being recognized for a change.

"I did?" Mrs. Hanahan put her purse on the counter. She opened it and began to rummage through it.

I knelt down. My knees reminded me that I was 63. I picked up the hundred that had landed right next to her brown shoe and then stood, trying not to wince. "This is what I think you dropped." I handed over the bill.

She looked at the hundred in my fingers and then up at me. She cackled. It was a lot louder than before. "If you think you can fool me with that trick, Mr. Williams, you've got another thing coming. I did not drop that. You did. I saw you do it while you were pretending to watch me sign my check."

I shrugged and continued to hold out the bill.

After two beats, she snatched it from my fingers and quickly dropped it in her purse. She then smartly snapped it closed and said, "And if you think I'm going to look a gift horse in the mouth, you've got yet another thing coming, *young man*."

Grinning, Isabel handed over the two fives and ten ones. "Here you go, Mrs. Hanahan."

"Thank you, my dear," replied the old woman, affectionately, as she took the money and then quickly opened her purse to drop it in. After she closed it right back up, she said, "It's always a pleasure to see you, Mrs. O'Malley. Please give your father my best regards."

"I will, Mrs. Hanahan."

Looking up at me, the old woman glared a little. "Take me for a fool, will you?" She harrumphed and then strode off across the store and towards the produce section. For a gal in her nineties, she had quite a bit of get-up-and-go.

Isabel burst out laughing. "That'll teach you, Nick." She leaned on the counter. "Little old ladies are always smarter than they look. And Mrs. Hanahan taught English at Mission High. I had her two years running and she was as sharp then as she is now."

I shrugged. "Well, I just—"

"You! Get outta my store!" That was Mr. Martinez and, even with my back turned to him, I knew he was talking to me.

"*Papi!*" said Isabel in a pleading tone as I turned to face the man. "He just told me about *Luis*."

Mr. Martinez was halfway between me and the front door. Carter was standing behind him with a face full of worry. Mr. Martinez was waving a cane in the air. I was convinced that it was a prop. "I don't care if he was here to take you to see the *pope*!" He pointed the cane at me. "I don't like you and I told you before that, if you came back again, I would call the police." As I grinned at him, he looked past me and said, "*Hija*! Call Sergeant *Gutierrez* at the precinct. Tell him to send the meanest cop they got."

Everyone in the store, of course, had stopped to watch what was going down. A couple of people laughed at his last sentence.

"You think I'm a crazy old man? Maybe I am. But I don't like you. You made my Doris into one of those lesbians."

"*Papi*! Doris was always a lesbian. We've talked about this before."

"I don't care," said Mr. Martinez, the distress on his face getting more and more obvious. "And now my *Luis* is gone." He pointed the cane at me. "Before you got here, we didn't have no gay Castro. It was Eureka Valley and nice, decent people lived there. Now it's full of all your people, including my *Luis*." His voice cracked. "And now he's gone and it's all your fault."

My grin had faded by then. The man was in a lot of pain.

Over his shoulder, I could see Carter making eyes towards the door. He wanted me to leave and I didn't blame him. I didn't want to stick around any longer myself, so I got the hell out of there and fast.

. . .

I looked at the machine, trying to figure out how it worked and whether it took hundreds or not. It didn't look like it did.

Wondering if maybe I should stop being a petulant punk and head back up the stairs, I watched as the African-American gal next to me inserted a five.

She glanced at me and then smiled as the machine spit out a ticket. "Never ride BART before?" she asked.

"No, ma'am."

She grinned. "You could be my grandfather, Mr. Williams. Where do you want to go?"

I grinned back. "Montgomery Street."

"That's where your office is, right?"

I nodded.

"Do you have anything smaller than a hundred?" she asked with a wink.

I shook my head. "Nope."

She reached into her over-the-shoulder purse, grabbed her wallet, and opened it up. Pulling out a one-dollar bill, she offered it to me. "Consider it a thank-you gift."

I took it. "For what?"

"My great uncle, who's gay, told me how you paid for his bail when he was arrested at a bar in Oakland back in the bad old days."

"Thank you."

"Sure." She watched me for a moment as I tried to figure out how to slide the dollar bill into the machine. "May I help you with that?"

I stepped back from the machine. "Please."

She shook her head. "No, sir. I teach kindergarten and one of the first things I learned from my mentor was to always walk my kids through a new task and to never do it for them."

"Smart."

"Now, just ease it into the machine from the edge. It'll catch it for you and then suck it in."

Instead of trying to push the bill in, which was what I'd been doing, I tried to follow her instructions. Sure enough, the machine sucked it in.

"Now, press this button."

I did that.

The machine thought for a moment and then made a noise. A white piece of cardboard, or something like that, popped out.

"Do I take that?" I asked.

"That's your ticket. Keep it. You'll need it to get out of the station at Montgomery."

"Thank you. I watched this thing being built for I don't know how long and have ridden it a few times, but never knew how to buy a ticket."

She pressed her lips together to keep from laughing as her black eyes danced with amusement. "Well, I'm glad to have been able to help."

"Where are you going?" I suddenly realized we were in the way, so I walked towards the place where people were inserting their tickets so they could walk through the gates.

"I'm headed to Embarcadero," she replied as she walked up to one of the gates and inserted her ticket. The panels opened and she stepped through. The panels closed and the machine popped her ticket out on the other end. She took it and then waited for me to do the same thing.

When I'd successfully gotten through, she led me towards a set of stairs that claimed to be leading to all trains. As we walked, she continued, "I'm meeting two of my aunts from Oakland and a cousin who's taking the Freedom Train up from San Jose. We're going to be in the parade today. Is your office open even though it's a holiday?"

We started down the steps.

I replied, "We're always open."

"What are you doing in this part of town?"

"I'm actually in the middle of throwing a fit because someone got mad at me."

She glanced at me while we walked down the stairs, side-by-side. "Trouble at home?"

I chuckled. "That's coming."

"Oh, I know what you mean by that."

"No, it's just that—" I stopped when we got to the bottom of the steps. "You don't want to hear all this."

"You'd be surprised," she replied as she made a U-turn around the stairs and led me towards one end of the platform. Pointing to an electronic sign that was flashing on the opposite side, she said, "That train is going to Daly City. We don't want to go there."

"It's Daly City. Why would we?" I asked, making the same joke I'd been making since I got home from the South Pacific.

She snorted as she pulled her purse under her arm and got it entangled a little bit in the wide sleeves of her brown and gold sweater. Once that was fixed, she looked at me. "You can tell me all about it. I'm a teacher of small children." She smiled. "I'm good at listening."

I sighed and then looked down at the tracks. "Well, we had to give a man the news that his nephew just died, and he blamed me."

"Suicide?"

I glanced at her. "AIDS."

She pressed her lips together again. "That sucks."

"Yeah."

We stood there for a moment as I looked at the tracks again.

"Where's your better half?"

"Steamed that I ran down the steps while he was shouting at me to stop."

She grinned. "Really? That sounds romantic."

"I guess. I just needed to clear my head." I blinked as the tears started coming again.

She sucked in her breath. "So many people..."

I nodded as I pulled out my handkerchief and dabbed my eyes. "Yeah. So many."

. . .

"So, are you going to watch the parade from your office?" That was Belinda, the gal who'd helped me buy my ticket and was sitting next to me on the train. She'd been telling me all about her kindergarten class up to that point.

"Nope. We're going to march. One of our friends asked us to and so we're meeting her at the office and then going from there."

She paused for a moment and then asked, "That wouldn't be Mrs. Geneva Watkins, would it?"

I looked at Belinda. "Yeah, as a matter of fact. Do you know her?"

"No..." She blinked. "Well, I know all about her, but I've never met her... At least not until later today. My Auntie Min—Mrs. Minnie Johnson is her name. She worked for Mrs. Watkins at the foundation before she retired."

"At the Bay Area Beneficial Foundation?"

She nodded. "I think Auntie Min knew your mother, too."

"Lettie was my stepmother. She's the one who started the foundation. Geneva took it over once she passed."

Belinda nodded as the train slowed down and a mechanical voice overhead announced that we were coming into the Montgomery Street station. "I guess we were destined to meet," she said. "Just not until later this morning."

I laughed as I stood. "I guess so. Thanks for your help."

She smiled at me. "Anytime. See you soon."

I nodded as the train stopped and the doors opened and I made my way onto the platform.

Chapter 3

Offices of WilliamsJones, Inc.
600 Market Street, Suite 3301
San Francisco, CA 94105
January 20, 1986
9:41 a.m. PST

I walked into Carter's office and plopped down on the sofa.

My husband, who was on the phone, took one disapproving look at me and then spun around in his chair so he could see the Ferry Building at the bottom of Market Street. After about five seconds, he said, "I don't care what they told you, I don't think Paramount is going to bid any higher." He sounded irritated. "Not that it's our problem. Let William Morris work it out." He waited for another few seconds. "I'll wait to hear from you. But I'm on board with another print run. Tell everyone in New York to get ready." He paused. "Thanks." He put the phone down but didn't turn to look at me.

"Hey there, fireman."

"Why didn't you come back up the stairs when I called you?" He was still looking out the window.

"Because I needed to clear my head."

Swiveling back around, his emerald green eyes bore into me. Leaning forward, he asked, "Nick, how many times do I have to tell you that we're in this together?"

I crossed my legs. "I don't not believe you." I shrugged. "I just needed to get away."

He scratched the back of his head. "On BART? Where were you gonna go? Fremont? Hayward?"

"I'm here, aren't I?"

He sighed and leaned back a little. "Yes, you are."

"Was that Bulworth?"

"Yep."

"Was that about *My Man*?"

"Yep."

"How much is Paramount offering?"

He gave me his half grin. "You promise Monumental isn't bidding?"

"Definitely. Ben doesn't think we can do it justice. How much? A hundred grand?"

He nodded and then looked down at his desk. He opened a folder and checked something. "We're on week five of being in the top five of the *Times'* list and we should be hitting number one by February."

I smiled. "Congratulations. How's the tour going?"

"Minnie seems to be having a blast, from what I hear. She's in Denver today." Minnie Roberts was the author of *My Man*. It was a fictionalized memoir of a 20s flapper from New York who ends up murdering her boyfriend, a Miami bootlegger.

I snapped my fingers. "Speaking of Minnie, you'll never guess who I met on BART."

He grinned. "Who?"

"Her first name is Belinda. She teaches kindergartners. And her aunt is Minnie Johnson."

His eyebrows shot up. "Minnie Johnson? Small world. She's a wonderful woman. Very funny."

"We'll see her later today, along with Belinda. I don't remember ever meeting Mrs. Johnson. Did we?"

He grinned. "We met her twice. Once at lunch at your father's apartment in 1974 and once at a big gala at the Mark Hopkins in 1981." Carter remembered everything.

I grinned back and then asked, "What time did Larry say he'd be bringing Geneva over?"

Carter looked at his watch. "They'll be here around 10:30." He then turned in his chair to look out the window. "We can watch the parade as it heads our way. And then we can go downstairs and join in as they pass by."

I stood and walked over to his chair. I kissed him on the top of his head and put both hands on his shoulders. "Sorry about ditching you, Chief. It was a lot to take, hearing Mr. Martinez say what he said."

He patted my hand and nodded. "I know, Nick. I know."

I kissed the top of his head again. "I love you."

He turned his chair around and then stood. Pulling me into his arms, he said, "I love you too."

. . .

"Hey, there, Nick, my man. How are you?" That was Lawrence "Larry" Roberts, a guy we'd first met when Carter and I had been arrested for loitering in Marin County back in '54. He offered his hand. I shook and then let him pull me in for a long hug.

I whispered in his ear, "It's always good to see you, Larry."

He pulled me in tighter in reply.

As we hugged, I could feel the tears coming to the surface again.

He sighed as he let go.

I stepped back to get a good look at him. He was African American, a little older than me but as handsome as ever. His head was covered with grey hair that he kept cut short. His skin was just about the blackest I'd ever seen, including when Carter and I lived in what had eventually become Zaire. On his left cheek, he had a long scar from a knife fight. He'd once told me it happened when some guy tried to pick up Sammy, his lover, back in the old days.

Carter, who'd been carefully hugging Geneva, said to her, "You look really wonderful."

Larry and I turned to watch the tall, handsome woman smile. "Thank you, Carter."

"When I'm your age," said Larry with a wicked smile that always made me go a little bit weak in the knees, "I hope I look that good."

She turned on him. "If you'd stop messin' around with men half your age, you just might live to be 78, Lawrence Roberts."

"Aw, Miss Geneva, don't knock it 'til you try it."

Carter and I both laughed at that. Even Geneva grinned a little.

She walked over towards the window next to Carter's desk. "I never tire of this view. I only wish we had some sunshine today."

Looking at her dark blue coat and skirt, I asked, "Do you think you'll be warm enough?"

She turned. "Oh, I left my coat in Larry's car. I'll be fine." With a slight frown, she looked over at the spiral staircase that led up to my office. "I don't suppose Miss Marnie is in today? Or did she take the day off?"

"Marnie has the flu and is at home," I replied. "She wanted to walk with us, but I put my foot down and told her to stay home and stay in bed." I added, somewhat wistfully, "Somebody's gotta do it."

Geneva's frown deepened. "I still can't believe Alex is gone. They were so much in love."

I nodded and tried not to cry for the umpteenth time that day. Alex LeBeau, Marnie's husband, had died a couple of years earlier. He'd had prostate cancer and the doctors found it too late to be able to do anything.

With a heavy sigh, Larry said, "Those boys half my age keep me young, Geneva." He walked over to the window and looked out. "I'm not afraid of dyin'. But I'm tired of watchin' everyone else die."

I couldn't argue with that.

Geneva, however, could and did. "You're 66, Larry Roberts. Did either of your folks live to be so old?"

He shook his head and quietly replied, "No, ma'am."

"I know mine didn't. Both mine were dead and buried by the time I turned 30." She walked over to him and took his arm. "Look out at the day and be glad that you're here to celebrate it. Did you ever think we would be walkin' up Market Street celebrating Dr. Martin Luther King?"

"No, ma'am."

Carter put his arm around my shoulder and pulled me in close.

"This is a glorious day," continued Geneva. "There's so much promise ahead. We both worked hard to get here, and I just can't have you tellin' me how bad it all is."

He sighed.

"I believe I was promised a cup of tea upstairs at David's. Which one of you handsome gentleman will be my escort?"

Before Carter or I could reply, Larry said, "I hope you'll allow me, Miss Geneva."

. . .

David's was the latest restaurant on the top floor of our building. They opened for lunch at 11, but David Baracci, the owner and chef, had promised we could go in early and sit at the table that was in the southeast corner of the building. That was the perfect spot to watch the parade as it headed up Market Street in our direction.

"I hope you have something warmer to wear, Mrs. Watkins." That was David. He was about 40, had a head full of curly black hair, and enough of a belly to grab Carter's attention. He'd trained as a chef in Paris with a woman named Simone Beck, whom Carter and I had met on a couple of occasions. After he'd opened his restaurant, the food critic for the *Examiner* had loved the food and described the place as being "like a Chez Panisse West with more pomp and less pretense," whatever the heck that meant.

Geneva reassured him she would be fine and then asked for a pot of Darjeeling tea and a plate of his orange Madeleine cookies, something he was famous for. Carter, Larry, and I asked for coffee. With that, David bowed, and walked off towards the kitchen.

"Goodness," said Geneva.

"What?" asked Carter.

"I just saw a patch of blue and some sunshine over Oakland."

Larry chuckled. "If you tell the sky to clear, Miss Geneva, I have no doubt it will do what you say." He looked at me and winked. "After all, you're one of the original Four Terrors."

Geneva preened just a little even as she said, "I do so dislike that name." She looked right at me when she said that.

I shrugged. "All I can say is that I was right. Besides, I once heard that when Governor Knight was told about that name, he'd vigorously agreed."

Larry stared at me for a moment. "So, that's the famous high-hat voice."

Nodding, Carter said, "It sure is."

A kid of about 25 showed up right then. He was carrying our coffees on a tray and handed them out with sugar and milk. Looking at Geneva, he said, "I'll be right back with your tea, Mrs. Watkins."

She smiled and said, "Thank you, Marc."

He nodded and walked off.

Answering my question before I could ask it, she said, "I know Marc through the foundation." She was a stickler for never talking about why she knew anyone that way, so I knew better than to ask.

Larry said, "I never did hear how you came up with that name, Nick."

I put two spoons of sugar in my coffee and then stirred as I grinned. "Well, it was when I saw Geneva, Lettie, Carter's mother, Louise, and her sister Velma all going after someone—"

"It was Rob-Rob," said Carter. That was Mayor Elmer Robinson.

I glanced at Geneva who was already shaking her head. Lips pursed, she said, "That man could glad hand all day long and well into the night, but he wasn't worth much as a mayor."

"He pretty much did what you wanted when it came to bulldozing the Western Addition, though," offered Carter.

She sniffed and looked ready to dive into one of her least favorite topics when Marc arrived and set out her tea.

"I'd give it one more minute to brew, Mrs. Watkins."

She smiled at him. "Thank you."

"The Madeleines will be ready in about five minutes."

"Thanks," said Carter with a grin.

Marc blushed. That only made sense. Carter was the most handsome man on seven continents. I knew because I'd checked.

Once the kid was gone, I looked over at Geneva and asked, "Did you work on the parade committee?"

Ignoring Marc's advice, she was pouring her tea right then. "No, sir, I did not." Once she'd put the pot back on the table, she added, "If there was to be a Fifth Terror, I'd nominate Reverend Cecil Williams for the job."

Carter and I both grinned and nodded while Larry chuckled. Cecil was the African-American pastor at Glide Memorial, a Methodist church in the Tenderloin. He was an activist and an organizer, and made all sorts of things happen for the community. Back before gay liberation, he'd helped out the kids in the Tenderloin and worked for gay rights. As soon as AIDS hit, he'd organized all manner of services for anyone who needed them.

We'd helped him out with different things over the years. But only when he would let us. He tended to shy away from anything that would brand him as being in bed with a capitalist. I couldn't blame him. If there was one thing I'd learned from being a reluctant billionaire, it was that sometimes money could solve a problem, but sometimes it made the problem worse. Cecil always knew where that line was. I respected and loved him for that and a whole lot more.

"Did the foundation do anything for the parade?" asked Larry.

"In part," replied Geneva, cryptically. Then, she quickly added, "Like anyone who's ever worked with him, I let Cecil tell me what he needs and let him handle his affairs in his way." She took a sip of tea. "I did hear, through the grapevine, that he made it clear to the folks in Atlanta that they should march in Atlanta and stay home."

"Why's that?" asked Larry, holding up his coffee cup and frowning over the rim at her.

She shrugged without replying and then looked at him. Her eyes were staring straight at him across the table and she was leaning forward just a little. I shivered since I knew that look. I'd been on the receiving end of it more than once. Larry was about to get a dressing-down.

"Mr. Roberts?"

His head was already bowed a little since he knew what was coming. "Yes, ma'am?"

"When are you going to take Sammy's ashes out to sea?" Samuel "Sammy" Johnson had been Larry's longtime lover. They'd been together almost as long as Carter and me. I considered them husbands, but neither liked that word. Sammy had passed away in the summer of '83. He'd had a heart attack in the middle of the night.

He lowered his eyes and put down his cup.

After a moment or two, Geneva asked, "Well?"

He looked up at her and then shrugged. "I just can't."

Reaching her long arm across the table, she took his hand in hers. "You won't be alone. We'll all be there with you." She squeezed his hand and, as if on cue, he started crying.

...

By the time the Madeleines arrived, Larry was looking out the window at the Ferry Building and the bay and saying, "Let's at least wait for it to warm up a little."

"I might not make it to September," said Geneva right before she took a tiny bite of her Madeleine.

We all looked at her. Carter asked, "Are you serious?"

"I'm going to turn 79 this year." She looked at the rest of her cookie. "Who knows how much longer I'll be around."

Larry shook his head. "Don't say that, Geneva."

She sighed a little, put her cookie on a plate, and then wiped her fingers with her napkin. "We're all going to die, Larry, even you."

He looked out the window and didn't say anything.

"My point is that it's time for you to say goodbye to Sammy. He'll always be with you, but there's a lot to be said about having a funeral or a wake. It helps the living. And you and Sammy have so many friends who would be glad to help you."

Carter and I both nodded at that.

Larry wiped a tear away with the back of his hand.

I had the feeling Geneva was talking to all of us when she added, "Life has to go on. We, the living, owe it to the ones who left us behind." That last part hit me hard. "It's time for you to move on. Sammy would want that."

I wanted to say something about how we could go out on our yacht, *The Serene Siren*, anytime he wanted, but it felt right to keep my mouth shut. Interrupting Geneva when she was on a roll was always a mistake.

After a long, tender moment, Larry nodded. "OK."

Carter quietly said, "We can go out on the *Siren* anytime you want. Just let us know." He then added, "Whenever you're ready."

Larry was nodding when Geneva said, "Goodness."

"What?" That was me.

"The parade is starting." Her voice cracked a little as she whispered, "For as hard as we worked to get here, I never thought this day would come." She blinked and then took the handkerchief that Carter offered her.

We watched in silence as the marchers began to file onto Market Street. By that time, the restaurant was open. People were beginning to trickle in for lunch.

As the marchers got closer and closer, I thought about Belinda down there and her two aunts who'd come in from Oakland and her cousin who'd taken the Freedom Train up from San Jose. That made me remember Mr. Martinez and Isabel and Luis. Then I wondered how Doris and Maria were holding up in Salinas.

I thought about the strange fact that the day, which was one for celebrating the work of a man who'd do so much for all of us, had, for me, been all about what every day had been about for too many years. All I wanted to do was to get through the pain and the dying and the suffering. And I knew I wasn't the only one. Far from it.

I glanced at Geneva. Her eyes were lit up and she was smiling. The expression on her face reminded me of the kind I'd seen on so many faces during that first Gay Freedom Day parade we'd attended back in the summer of '73. I was happy that she was happy. But I couldn't help but feel a sadness—

Stop. I had to stop. We were celebrating Dr. King. I looked out the window. There were thousands of people marching up Market and getting closer and closer.

That was what was happening. That was what was real.

Carter, who was sitting next to me, took my hand right then. I wondered if he could tell I was brooding.

Glancing at his emerald eyes, I felt the sadness lift a little.

His sweet, sweet smile reminded me of the rich tapestry of love and desire and friendship between us. It reminded me of the love that we shared with Geneva and Larry and so many of the people we knew.

Looking out the window again, I began to feel the heaviness of the morning lift a little bit more. All those people out on the street were marching for freedom and celebrating one of the many people who'd helped make it happen. I decided, right then, that I would make that the most important thing, at least for the day.

Tomorrow, Tuesday, would arrive soon enough.

But it was Monday and not even noon. It was a day for celebration. Yes, it was. And I was determined to do just that. Yes, I was.

One of the waiters stopped by. For whatever reason, he put his hand on my shoulder as he took a long look out the window. That one gesture of solidarity, whether that was his intent or not, took me by surprise. It was nothing and yet it said everything.

Suddenly, I was ready to go downstairs and get out on the street and be with the people who were probably laughing and singing and enjoying the powerful feeling of being together.

Removing his hand, the waiter said, "It's like a pride parade down there."

"But without the drag queens," added a woman at the table next to us.

Geneva replied, "I wouldn't be too sure of that."

"Me, neither," said Larry as we all laughed.

Finally, we were too high up to see the banner which had read:

Living The Dream
Martin Luther King, Jr.
First National Holiday
Jan. 20, 1986

Geneva put her napkin on the table and said, "Let's go down and join everyone."

The four of us stood. I pushed a hundred in Marc's hand as we walked by him and made our way to the elevator.

As the doors closed and the car started its way down to the parking garage, Geneva said, "I want all of you to remember what this day is about."

It was a command—not a suggestion.

"We worked hard to get here." She turned around, looked at me, and then up at Carter. "All of us. Do you hear me?"

Carter and I both nodded as he said, "Yes, ma'am."

Turning back around to face the door, she continued, "So, when we go out there and join all our friends, remember what we did to get here and what Martin did and all those who're gone but who made today possible. I don't want to see anyone crying. I want you to sing and thank the Lord and look around and see what can happen when you organize and make a real and abiding change. Do you understand me?"

"Yes, ma'am," replied the three of us as the door opened to the little lobby just outside the garage.

"Did you hear that?" asked a woman walking past us to get on the elevator we were getting off of.

"What?" said her companion, also a woman. They were both wearing jeans and thick sweaters and looked to be in their 30s. I'd seen them before and was pretty sure they worked at our computer division down in Burlingame.

"They're singing."

She was right.

We could hear the voices floating in from the street as Carter held the door to the garage open for us.

We shall overcome
We shall overcome
We shall overcome, some day

Oh, deep in my heart
I do believe
We shall overcome, some day

St. Valentine's Day 1951

Chapter 1

137 Hartford Street
San Francisco, Cal.
Tuesday, February 13, 1951
Just past dawn

I opened my eyes. The light in the room was dim but the sun was up. And the room was freezing. Someone had stolen all the covers and I was cold. I rolled off the frigid bed and made my way into the bathroom. The tile was cold on my feet. As I did my business, I remembered that, starting at 4 that afternoon, Carter would be working a forty-eight hour shift at the firehouse, Station Three to be precise.

Carter Jones was my lover of about three and a half years. He was tall, standing at 6'4", and muscular with sandy-blond hair and a ruddy complexion. He was from South Georgia and talked like you'd expect. I loved him even if he did tend to steal the covers on a cold February morning.

As I waited for the hot water tap in the bathtub to deliver the goods, I sighed as I worried, one more time, about what to give him for Valentine's Day. He would be working all that day, so it was going to have be Friday, the 15th, before we could do anything. The obvious choice was to take him for dinner at the Top of the Mark, a swank joint at the top of the Mark Hopkins Hotel on Nob Hill. But I wanted to do something more than just dinner. I wanted to give him something to let him know how much I loved him.

By the time the hot water heater began to crank out, I could hear the springs creak a little in the bedroom.

"Damn, son, it's freezing in here."

"How would you know?"

As he padded into the bathroom with a sleepy grin, he said, "Sorry 'bout that." He started doing his business as I plugged the hole at the bottom of the ancient cast-iron bathtub. I walked over to the gas heater that sat in the corner and lit it. I sat on my haunches and held my cold hands in front of the gas flame in an attempt to warm them up.

Carter flushed, walked over to the sink, and washed his hands. He asked, "You first?"

I stood. "Sure."

We both slept in the buff, so I walked to the side of the tub, lifted my left leg over, and gingerly put my foot in the tub, testing the water as I did. It was perfect. Once I was in, I stretched out and looked up at the man I loved. He was grinning down at me. His hair was pointing in every direction.

I looked down at the water and then back up at him. "You gonna help me out here?"

Smirking, Carter walked over to the side of the tub and squatted. Reaching across me and taking the tube of Perl from the little shelf by the tub, he looked at it for a moment. "I've never understood why you like this stuff."

"It's green. And it smells good. Don't you want my hair to be radiantly clean?" I tried to say that last part as dead-pan as I could.

He rolled his eyes, put his big right hand on the top of my head, and asked, "Ready?"

I held my breath as he pushed me down into the sloshing bath water and ran his hand through my hair to rinse out the previous day's mass of pomade. Once that was done, I sat up and wiped the water off my face with my hands.

"See, this is why I don't like baths. Now you're sitting in warm water and pomade." He unscrewed the shampoo tube and, holding it over my head, squirted a little on top.

"I'm still cold."

He didn't reply as he began to rub the shampoo into my hair, creating a lather as he did. The bathroom filled with the aroma of the green shampoo. I'd never been able to figure out if it was supposed to be grass or flowers or what. But whatever it was, I liked it.

After a moment, Carter said, "OK, down you go." He pushed down on my head as I held my breath and slid under the water. Using both of his hands, he rinsed my hair off.

Once that was done, I sat back up and sputtered the water away from my face. He stood, handed me a fresh washcloth, and said, "You're on your own, son. I'm headed downstairs to put on the percolator."

I took the square piece of cotton and, looking significantly at the water, said, "You're missing the best part."

He grinned down at me. It was obvious he was interested. "What about coffee?"

I shrugged. "It can wait."

He grinned and squatted down again. "I was thinking about Mildred's for breakfast anyhow."

As he reached down into the murky water to clean the most important place on a man's body, I sighed contentedly and replied, "Yeah, that's good."

Chapter 2

Mildred's Diner
Corner of Ellis and Van Ness
Tuesday, February 13, 1951
Just past 8 in the morning

"Table in the back is free, fellas." That was Mildred, the owner of the joint. She was a thin gal with a Texas-sized personality. The place was slammed, mostly at the counter. I followed Carter as he made his way through the place and back to our usual spot. It was the table closest to the kitchen and rarely in use, unless it was a Sunday morning before church services started or a Saturday morning most anytime.

I plopped down in the chair that faced the kitchen while Carter took his usual seat giving him a view of the diner. He handed me the *Chronicle* while he kept the *Examiner* for himself, which was fine by me. I didn't much care for Hearst and his politics.

"Well, look what the cat dragged in!" Mildred walked up with a coffee pot in her hands. She grinned down at us. "Coffee, fellas?"

Neither of us had turned over our cups, so we did just that. She expertly filled them both without missing a drop. Putting her coffee pot on the Formica tabletop, she pulled out an order pad from her skirt and a pencil from inside her hairdo. "What'll it be?"

Carter replied, "Three eggs over easy, hashed brown potatoes, and a ham steak."

As she wrote, she said, "Goin' easy on the vittles this mornin', are ya Red?"

Carter laughed. "I guess you could add a side of chewy bacon."

"Toast?"

"Buttered white, please, ma'am."

She nodded and then looked at me. "What about you, Slim?"

"Two scrambled eggs, chewy bacon, and buttered rye toast."

"Got it. It'll be out in a minute." She picked up her coffee pot and swayed her hips on her way to the kitchen door. Once she got there, she called out, "Three cackleberries over easy, spike on an oval, pig on a platter, side of rashers on a dare." She waited as the cook mumbled something in reply. Then she continued, "Wreck two with rashers on a dare." The cook called back to her to the sound of grease splattering and that was that.

. . .

"Looks like *All About Eve* is going to sweep the Oscars." That was Carter.

I glanced up from a story I was reading about some poor kid down in L.A. who'd decided it would be a good idea to drop a lit match down the gas tank of his father's car. "Good. I liked that movie." We'd seen it a couple of times since it came out.

Carter folded his paper and had a sip of coffee. He leaned forward. "I still believe that George Sanders and Eve are playing homosexuals."

It was a silly argument we'd been having since the first time we'd seen the movie. I suspected that Carter brought it up to get a rise out of me.

I sighed. "Nope. Eve is as red-blooded as Bette Davis and Karen. Remember? He tells her that he owns her. That's what they do."

"What do you mean?"

"You know. You work with plenty of 'em. Those red-blooded men who *own* their girlfriends and wives. Just ask Carlo Martinelli." That was a fireman who worked with Carter.

Right then, Mildred walked up and set down our plates. Once that was done, she asked, "How's the coffee, fellas?"

I replied, "I'll take a bump."

Carter nodded. "Same for me. Thanks, Mildred."

"Sure thing, Red." She sauntered off to find her coffee pot as we dug into our breakfast.

Carter started cutting into his ham steak. As he did, he looked at me. "I thought you said that Carlo was one of us."

"Mack said that," I replied as I bit into a slice of bacon. Mack had been a lover of mine and had been killed over in Korea the year before. He'd claimed that Martinelli had to be one of us because he talked about his female conquests non-stop. "I'm more Switzerland on the matter."

Carter snorted as Mildred returned and began to top up our coffee. She asked, "What's so funny, Red?"

"Pipsqueak over there just said something funny."

She looked down at me and shook her head. "Did I ever tell you two about Shorty?"

I grinned, knowing a good story was coming. "Nope."

"Well, we knew each other back in Texas and—"

Right then, there was a tremendous crash from somewhere behind me along with a kid's squeal.

Mildred was off in a dash, muttering, "Damn kids."

Without turning around, I asked Carter, "What happened?"

He smiled indulgently, like he always did where kids were concerned. "A toddler just threw a plate of scrambled eggs on the floor. It broke into about six pieces."

I grinned. "Poor Mildred."

He wolfed down half a piece of his toast. "Back to Carlo."

"Yeah?"

"I've never once heard him say anything like that. It's the married guys who talk that way. Particularly that slob, Tony Kellerman."

"The one who lives up on Portola?"

"That's the one. I'd like to take him out back one of these days and teach him a lesson."

"He still beating up on his wife?"

Carter nodded. "The part that's the worst is that the cops won't do anything."

"Why doesn't she leave him?"

"From what Kellerman says, they live on his salary and barely get by. I don't think she has any family."

"See? That's what I mean. He *owns* his wife. What's her name?"

He sighed. "Georgia."

"Have you ever met her?"

He shook his head. "None of us have. You know how

some of the guys have cookouts at their houses? Kellerman never has."

I snorted. "Neither has Fireman Jones."

He pursed his lips and narrowed his eyes. "Nick..." He used about three syllables to get his point across.

I held out my hands in surrender. "I know, I know." I had never once asked him what he told the other firemen about his home life. I knew he probably had a story, but I didn't want to know. I took a sip of my coffee and asked, "Did you ever talk to your captain about Kellerman?"

Carter picked at his hashed brown potatoes. "Yes, but he says there's nothing he can do. There's no rule about firemen not beating their wives."

I nodded thoughtfully.

Chapter 3

777 Bush Street
Third Floor
Tuesday, February 13, 1951
A quarter past 9 in the morning

I walked through the front door of the outer part of the office and said, "Morning."

Marnie Wilson, my secretary, looked up from her desk where she was knitting and said, "Good morning, Nick. How are you?"

I replied, "Fine," as I made my way to the back office. I put my hat and overcoat on the rack and walked back to Marnie's desk. "Anything on the books for today?"

She slowly shook her head. "Nothin' so far. You got that one case at the St. Francis Hotel, but I ain't heard back from the clerk you paid off. He's supposed to call when Mr. Weathersby checks in."

I nodded. "How's the sweater coming?"

She held up a small square of knitted dark green yarn. "I finished that one yesterday. This is a new scarf for Mother."

"How is she?"

She sighed. "Same as always."

I pulled over the chair that I used for clients and sat next to her desk. "I have a problem I want your help with."

Her eyes lit up. "Yeah? What is it?"

"What to get Carter for Valentine's Day."

She sighed. "Oh."

I laughed. "You thought it was gonna be real work, right?"

She nodded. "Yeah. I've been working for you for what? Four, five months? I know it's kinda weird to wanna actually do something for all the dough you're payin' me just to sit here and knit, but I guess that's how I am." She sighed loudly, put her needles and yarn on the desk, and looked at me. "OK. How about dinner tomorrow night at the Top of the Mark? I'm sure you can wave some money under the nose of that snooty French maitre d' and get a table, even on Valentine's Day."

"Carter's shift starts today at 4 and he doesn't get off until 8 on Friday morning."

She frowned. "Then why are you here, for Pete's sake?"

I shrugged. "I think he's out getting something for me. He took the Buick and dropped me off here. Told me not to go home until noon."

She nodded. "Makes sense. You two seem to be joined at the hip except when he's at the station." She narrowed her eyes for a moment. "OK. What about a car? Do you think he wants his own car?"

I smiled. "I already tried to give him a car a couple of times. He says we don't need two. The garage will only hold the Buick. And he doesn't mind taking the streetcar down Market to get to and from work."

She put her left hand to her chin. "Yeah. He's like that. What about the usual? Flowers?"

"Since I'm not allowed to go to the firehouse, I'd thought about arranging for a flower delivery van to crash out front. Right there on Post."

Marnie giggled and said, "Oh, Nick."

"Not too practical, right?"

"Nope." She thought for a moment before asking, "What does the man who can buy anything get for the man who doesn't want anything?"

"Is that how you see us?"

She nodded. "Yeah. You could *buy* the St. Francis and put a big bow on it. But what would a fireman do with a hotel?"

"But do you think he really doesn't want anything?"

She shrugged. "You just told me how he doesn't want his own car. You also told me when I first started working for you in October how you'd told him how you'd be happy living on his salary. I thought that's why you never spend any of your own dough."

I sighed. "Truth is that I don't know what to do with it. It's not really mine. I didn't earn it."

She sat back and crossed her arms. "I never heard of any rich guy saying anything like that before."

I shrugged. "But that's the way it is."

"Why don't you give it away?"

"I have a foundation. They do that."

"You do?"

I nodded. "I guess I never told you. Jeffery Klein set it up back in '49." That was my lawyer and an old lover. He worked down the street at the Shell Building. Besides handling my legal work, he also defended a lot of the guys and gals who got caught up in the police raids that, from time to time, swept through the nightclubs of the sort that people like us tended to frequent.

Marnie looked down at her yarn and sighed. "Nick, why don't you let me be a real secretary?"

"How so?"

"You can have all your mail sent here. I can sort it out for you. That sort of thing."

I shrugged. "I'll have to tell Jeffery—"

"See, Nick? I can call Klein for you. And tell him whatever you need me to." She sighed. "You could give me something to do besides knit." With a small smile, she added, "That would be a swell Valentine's Day present."

I grinned. "Sure thing. You tell me whatever you think I should do."

Her eyes lit up. "Well, I have a—"

I held up my right hand. "First things first. What about Carter?"

She nodded. "Right." She thought for a moment. "Is there something you could do *for* him that doesn't mean buying something for him?"

"Like what?"

"I dunno." She thought for a moment. "You could send his folks some cash, maybe."

I shook my head. "Nope."

"Are his folks dead?"

"Dead to him is more like it."

"Long story?"

I nodded. "Yeah. I'll tell you some other time. His mother—" I snapped my fingers. "Hey! I've got an idea."

"You do?"

"Yeah." I told her about Tony Kellerman and his wife, Georgia.

When I was done, her eyes were blazing. "It's a good thing my mother isn't here to hear about this. What a no-good son of a bitch!"

I sat back. She was right. But I'd never heard her talk like that before. "I could do something to help *her*."

She nodded. "Is he on the same shift as Carter?"

"Yeah."

She thought for a moment. Finally, she waved me away, saying, "You go on home. If I hear from the St. Francis, I'll call you. Otherwise, I'll see you at 4. When you get here, I'll have a plan."

I grinned. "Sounds good."

She nodded. "I have an idea already but I wanna run some of it by Mother. She's smart like that."

"Am I ever gonna get to meet your mother?"

She shrugged. "When I get to meet your father, I guess."

I snorted. "That's never gonna happen. Besides, I thought you were close to your mother."

She rolled her eyes. "Only because I have to be since she lives with me." Sighing, she added, "Mother's problem is that she really oughta been born a man. If she was really let loose, she'd give that General MacArthur a real run for his money."

Chapter 4

Walking down Bush Street
Tuesday, February 13, 1951
Half past 10 in the morning

I knew Carter had some sort of Valentine scheme up his sleeve, but I had no idea what it might be. Whatever it was, it would happen between noon and half past 3. That was when he had to be on his way to work to make it to the firehouse by 4.

Since Marnie had kicked me out of my own office and Carter wasn't going to let me into my own house, I decided to go for a walk down Bush Street and see what Jeffery was up to. I'd seen him the week before and he was in the middle of a messy break-up with Adam, another lawyer he knew. They'd been going together since New Year's Eve when they'd met but it wasn't working out. I wanted to find out the latest and see if he'd started putting on weight yet. He usually did when he wasn't getting any action in the bedroom.

I had just crossed the Stockton Street Tunnel and was walking past the Welfare Department office when I saw a woman exit a phone booth. She was in her 30s, had a worried expression, and was wearing an old black wool coat that was fraying at the cuffs. As she passed me, her head down and frowning, I thought about Marnie and had an idea. I pulled a hundred out of my wallet, folded it over, and turned around.

The woman was slowly making her way up Bush. I ran towards her and called out, "Miss?"

She stopped and looked at me. "Yes?"

"I think you dropped something in that phone booth."

She shook her head as she opened her pocketbook, which was a shoddy old leather job and heavily wrinkled. "I don't think so."

"Really?" I handed across the folded hundred. "I found this on the floor of the phone booth."

She looked at it and then up at me. "What is this?"

"It's a hundred. And it's not mine."

She shook her head. "Well, it's not mine. I've never seen one of those in my life."

I shrugged and held it out. "It has to be yours. You were the last one in there."

She narrowed her eyes at me. "Is this some sort of gag, mister?"

"Gag?"

"Sure. Maybe that's counterfeit and you're trying to pass it off."

I shrugged. "Nope. I just wanna make sure you get your property." I pushed it a little further in her direction. "Seems like no one can afford to pass up a hundred."

She looked at me. "Then why don't you keep it?"

"It isn't mine."

She shrugged. "I don't know what to tell you." With that, she turned away and continued to trudge up the street.

I stuck the bill in my trouser pocket and wondered about that. When I'd been a kid, my sister and I had given dollar bills and quarters from our allowances to the men we saw on the street who were obviously down on their luck. We'd lived in a big mansion on Nob Hill and our father gave us five bucks a month as an allowance, which was a lot of money in those days. But, once he'd found out what we were doing, he'd cut it back to a dollar each and given us a long lecture about knowing the value of money and how those men, in the depths of the Depression, could get a job if they really wanted one. He'd always been a miserable S.O.B. and that instance more than amply proved so.

. . .

As I walked into the plush offices of one Jeffery Klein, Esquire, on the tenth floor of the Shell Building, I was happy to see Robert, his cute and all-smiles receptionist, busy at the phone.

He smiled at me, held up his right finger, and continued with his conversation. "That's right. We're trying to find a Samuel Gustafson. He's supposed to be at the Central Station, but they can't seem to find him. They suggested calling Mission, so that's why I'm talking to you." He listened to whoever was on the other end while I stood and looked around. Jeffery liked swank and he was doing pretty good business. The office had deep pile carpeting and was nicely furnished.

Right then, Robert said, "I see, Sergeant. I'll try that, then. Thank you for your time." He put the phone down and smiled up at me. "How are you, Mr. Williams?"

"Fine, Robert. How goes it with you?"

"Good enough. He's free. Should I let him know you're here?"

I shook my head. "No. Lemme surprise him."

He smiled. "You're the only one who's allowed to, so go right in."

I lifted my hat. "Thanks, kid."

. . .

As I sat back in the deep leather chair, I said, "You look good, Jeffery."

He was standing at a filing cabinet and looking for something in one of the drawers that was reserved for my legal affairs. Apparently, I got an entire cabinet— four drawers, in fact. Jeffery stood around 6'1", had brown hair and brown eyes, and was handsome enough. When he was in love, he was fit and trim. Otherwise, he tended to put on weight.

We'd met by telegram and letter when a Navy commander I was serving under during the war had suggested him as a lawyer who could help me with the sudden inheritance that had fallen into my lap in '44. Jeffery and I had met in person not long after Mack and I split which was as soon as we got back to San Francisco once the war was over. I'd moved from Mack's loving arms into Jeffery's indifferent ones. We were good friends but had been lousy lovers. I'd met Carter about the time I'd decided to break things off with Jeffery and, so far, Carter and I were living happily ever after.

Jeffery found the folder he was looking for, slammed the drawer closed, and collapsed into his big desk chair. Behind him, I could see the gleaming blue waters of the San Francisco Bay. It was quite a view.

Sighing heavily, he said, "Adam and I are back on." Looking up from the folder, he added, "At least until tomorrow night. I hate being alone on Valentine's Day."

I leaned forward. "You got back together with this guy because you don't wanna be alone tomorrow night?"

Jeffery nodded without replying. He looked at the folder and paged through until he found whatever he was looking for. "I need you to sign this. There's a new board member on the foundation and they want to expand—"

I waved him away. "You think I should sign it?"

He nodded. "Yes. It would be—"

"Gimme a pen."

He sighed as he pushed the page across his desk and unscrewed a fountain pen. "One of these days, Nick..."

"Yeah, yeah." I put my John Hancock on paper and then pushed the thing back at him.

He blotted the page and put it in a box on the corner of his desk. As if he'd suddenly realized I was in the room, he looked up at me and frowned. "What are you doing here? Why aren't you at work?"

"Nothing to do. Besides, I'm killing time until I'm allowed to go home."

Jeffery raised an eyebrow at me. "*Allowed*?"

I nodded. "Yeah. Carter told me not to come home until noon." I looked at my watch. It was a few minutes past 11. I had another fifteen minutes before I needed to get on a streetcar down on Market Street.

"Why's that?"

"I'm guessing he's doing something for Valentine's Day. He goes in at 4 and doesn't get off until 4 on Thursday afternoon."

Jeffery nodded as he bit the inside of his mouth.

I asked, "So, does Adam know this is why you're holding on?"

He shook his head, looking guilty.

"Look, why don't you and me go out tomorrow night? I can slip the maitre d' some cash and get us a swell table at the Old Poodle Dog or the Fairmont."

He gave me half a smile. "Why not the Top of the Mark?"

I shrugged but didn't reply.

"Oh, so that's where you're going on Thursday night with Carter, is it?"

I nodded. "Come on, Jeffery. You don't wanna go out with Adam tomorrow night. And you won't be alone."

He took a deep breath and seemed to think about it. Finally, he gave me a small smile. "Can I call you later?"

I grinned. "Sure."

"You're always so good to me, Nick. Sometimes I wonder why."

"'Cause I love you, Jeffery. Why else?"

Chapter 5

137 Hartford Street
Tuesday, February 13, 1951
Right at noon

I pressed on the doorbell and waited. After a few seconds, I heard a pair of size 14 feet stomp across the living room floor.

Carter opened the door, reached out, and pulled me in by my tie, slamming the door behind as soon as I was across the threshold.

He then pulled me in close and kissed me deeply for a long while. Once we came up for air, I realized he was wearing his fireman gear. Or, rather, the part of his uniform that he wore underneath the protective parts.

He had on a dark blue t-shirt over a pair of white BVDs. He was bare-legged down to his thick gray socks which, as always, appeared too small for his feet and yet sagged at his ankles. I looked up and realized he was also wearing his hat with a big "3" emblazoned on the front.

"What's all this, fireman?" I asked with a grin.

He wiggled his eyebrows down at me. "You told me you liked this getup."

I laughed. "I do." I stepped back and looked down at his legs, appreciating their muscled features and the fact that they were covered in golden red hair. "It shows off your legs to their best advantage."

He pulled my hat off and tossed it over on the sitting room sofa.

"So that's how it's gonna be?" I asked.

He nodded slowly. "Yeah. But first, I'm gonna feed you some lunch. Then..." He turned and padded his way to the kitchen.

I followed him, undoing my tie as I did. "Then what?"
"You'll find out."

As we entered the kitchen, I stopped. The round table at the end of the room was covered in white linen. It looked odd in the bright light of the noonday sun, but I loved it. A silver candelabra sat in the middle. All the candles were blazing. On the table were small plates and little bowls full of different things.

"What's this?" I asked.

He turned and stood in front of me. "Lunch. Now, let's get you more comfortable, Mr. Private Dick."

I grinned and shed my coat. He took that and finished pulling off my tie. Snapping his fingers, he said, "Now for the shirt. It's undershirts only for this meal." Once I was done with that, he said, "Now, kick off your shoes." I complied with a grin.

He leaned over, picked them up, and said, "Now go have a seat and I'll be right back."

I did what he said, having a quick qualm about being caught by the open windows until I remembered that our neighbors, Pam and Diane, were both at work. They were the only two who could see into the kitchen and only from their upstairs guest bedroom, so we were fine.

I sat down at the table and looked at the bowls and plates. There were shelled almonds, whole strawberries, bits of chocolate, a small bowl of honey, a plate of sliced lemons, and little red berries I'd never seen before. There was also a small unlabeled bottle of red sauce of some sort.

Right then, Carter padded back in. He was still wearing his fire engine hat. Walking over to the counter, he picked up a small knife. He then opened the icebox and reached into the freezer. He pulled out a bowl of something and wandered over to the table. As he put the bowl down, I realized it held a dozen unshucked oysters. That was what the knife was for.

He pulled a chair around the table and sat down in front of me. Pulling himself close and to the point where my knees touched the upper part of his hairy shins, he said, "This is my little love lunch for you, son."

I grinned. "Are these all the aphrodisiacs?"

He nodded. "All the ones I could get my hands on, Spanish Fly still being unavailable." He pulled an oyster out of the bowl and, using the knife, he expertly opened one.

"How'd you learn to do that?" Carter generally despised seafood. I figured he'd never shucked an oyster in his life.

"Practice, son." He looked at the table. "You want hot sauce or lemon juice?"

I shrugged.

"How do you usually eat them?" he asked.

"Lemon juice," I replied.

"Let's try something hot and spicy." He said that without laughing, which was impressive. He opened the little bottle with the red sauce and sprinkled the open oyster with a couple of red drops. "Open wide, Nick."

I did as he said and swallowed the oyster. It burned a little as it went down, but it wasn't bad.

"Oh, shit," said Carter, jumping up and bumping the table as he did. The candelabra wobbled a little but didn't fall over. A couple of almonds rolled out of their dish. Carter reached down and picked one up. He ran it through the honey and then reached over and held it to my lips.

I opened up and let him stick the whole thing into my mouth. I closed my lips over his fingertips and licked off the honey. His fingers tasted like oyster juice underneath. I looked up at him and smiled as he pulled his fingers back. He leaned down and kissed me, using his tongue to take the almond out of my mouth. He then stood, chewed it, and swallowed it with a grin.

I kept smiling but wasn't sure I liked feeding him like a mother bird.

He bounced over to the icebox and pulled out a split of champagne, beginning to unwrap it.

"You have to work tonight."

He nodded. "I know, but you don't."

I shook my head. "Actually, I do."

He sighed, opened the icebox door, and put the bottle back in. "Sorry. What about a Coke?"

I looked down at the strawberries and shook my head. "How about milk?"

He snorted. "Milk?"

"Sure."

He nodded and walked over to the cabinet. Pulling down two small glasses, he put them on the counter and then walked back to the icebox. Opening the door, he pulled out a bottle of milk. He removed the paper cover and poured out two glasses. After replacing the cover, he put the bottle of milk back in the icebox.

He then padded over with the two glasses. As he sat down, he bumped the table again, and spilled the milk of the glass in his left hand on my trousers.

He whispered, "Shit," and put both glasses on the table. As I watched, trying very hard not to laugh, he walked back to the counter and picked up a towel. He carefully sat down in front of me and tried to blot the milk off the wool of my trousers.

Once that was done, he flung the towel over to the counter. As he did, the edge of it brushed past one of the candles and caught fire, landing on the tablecloth as it did.

We both stood at the same time. He bonked his head on mine. It sounded like two coconuts banging together.

Carter said, "Damn!" as I reeled back, holding my head where he hit it and trying not to fall on my ass.

Being the fireman that he was, Carter dumped the milk from both glasses on the towel and quickly smothered the flame with his hands. He then licked his right index finger and, with his right thumb, rapidly extinguished each candle.

Once that was done, we both looked at each other and burst out laughing. His emerald green eyes sparkled as he did, and I could feel myself falling in love with him even more than I ever remembered falling before.

He pulled me close and said, "Sorry for almost burning down the house, son."

I dug my face into the hard pillow of his chest and said, "It's all those goddam aphrodisiacs."

...

"Try this. Don't bite down. Just suck." That was Carter as he popped two of the little red berries in my mouth.

I was stretched out on our bed, while he sat next to me, with a small tray between us. We were both buck naked. His engine hat was lying next to the tray.

We'd decided that was a better place to continue having lunch. And it was.

I sucked the slightly sour, slightly sweet flesh off of each seed and then spit them out into my right hand. Carter offered a small dish and I let them fall into it. "What are those?" I asked.

"Pomegranates," replied Carter.

I sat up on my elbow and poked at one of the small seeds in the dish. "That's a pomegranate?"

"Well, it's the seed inside one. Those are damn hard to get into, I'll tell you that." He then offered me a strawberry. Like I'd been doing, I grabbed his fingertips with my lips. He seemed to like it. I knew that I did.

"This is the best lunch I've ever had," I said as he dabbed the side of my face to get the strawberry juice off.

"I love you, Nick."

I nodded and looked up at him. "I love you, too, Carter."

He leaned over and kissed me deeply for a long moment.

. . .

When I opened my eyes, I looked at my watch. It was a few minutes past 4. I jumped up and called out, "Carter?"

Getting no reply, I looked around. The bed was clear of all the dishes we'd brought upstairs. The tray was gone, as well. I could feel a panic rising up inside of me. Where was he? What had happened?

I jumped out of bed and raced down the stairs. "Carter?" Still getting no reply, I ran into the kitchen and stopped. All evidence of our earlier meal was gone. The table was bare, and all the chairs had been put back in place. I opened the icebox and relaxed a little. The split of champagne was still there. The rest of the pomegranate berries were on a plate with the leftover strawberries and almonds. I reached in and grabbed two almonds. Closing the door, I popped them both in my mouth and very slowly chewed them, remembering the taste of Carter's honey-covered fingers that were mingled with oyster juice.

I walked over to the cabinet below the counter where we kept the garbage pail, opened it, and found more evidence of what we'd been up to earlier. Empty oyster shells were mixed with white pomegranate seeds and the green tops of strawberries in the paper bag we lined the pail with. For some reason, that made me feel better.

I stood in the kitchen, buck naked, and wondered at the panic I'd briefly felt. I was convinced, for one very terrifying moment, that I'd dreamed up Carter's sweet aphrodisiac lunch.

I then realized I was late getting back to the office. Walking over to the phone alcove, I picked up the phone receiver and dialed the office number. After a couple of rings, Marnie answered, "Private investigator, may I help you?"

"It's Nick."

"Where are you?"

"I just woke up from a nap."

"A nap?"

"Yeah. I'll explain later. I'll be there in about thirty minutes."

"Nick?"

"Yeah?"

"Why don't I come to your house?"

"Sure. You remember where it is?"

"Oh, sure."

"Take a cab and let yourself in if I don't answer."

"OK. Be sure to put on your very best clothes."

I laughed. "Will do." I paused and then added, "Sorry, Marnie. I hate being late."

She giggled. "I suppose this has something to do with Carter's Valentine Day's gift for you?"

"And how."

. . .

I had just finished tying my tie when the doorbell rang. I pulled on my coat and hopped down the stairs, taking two at a time. When I got to the bottom, I grabbed my hat from the sofa where Carter had tossed it earlier, and then made my way to the front door.

I pulled it open and said, "Come on in."

She hesitated, looking around me. "Are you sure, Nick?"

I nodded. "Come on in. It's just me."

That seemed to relax her for some reason. I wondered if she was intimidated by Carter. He was mighty tall and wide. But he was usually very sweet and polite, particularly with the gals. The two had only met three or four times. Then I realized that the only other time Marnie had been to the house, I'd asked her to wait outside while I got my coat and hat. That had been because we were in a hurry and I knew I wouldn't have time to show her the house, if she'd wanted to see it.

I knew I was the first homosexual she'd ever really met or spent any time with. She'd never asked me the usual awkward questions, like who was the wife, or that kind of nonsense. But she'd always been very quiet and circumspect around the homosexual clients I'd worked for. That was in contrast to how she acted with the females, the straight ones. She was usually gregarious and welcoming.

As she walked in, I asked, "Wanna have a look around?" I had no idea if she would, but I thought it would be polite, particularly if she had the idea that it was a place I didn't want her to see for whatever reason she might have cooked up.

She looked at her watch. "Maybe some other time. If we're gonna do this, we need to leave pretty soon."

"Do what?" I asked.

She giggled. "Oh, right. I haven't told you the plan."

I smiled and waited.

"Well, it involves going to see Mrs. Kellerman. Mother had a brilliant idea and I think it might just work. We need to take your car, of course." She frowned slightly. "You do have it, right?"

I nodded. "I think. I was asleep when Carter left. But he almost always takes the streetcar."

"Good." She waited.

"Don't we need to look up—?"

"1406 Portola. Looked it up in Polk's."

I nodded. "OK. Let's go."

. . .

The Buick easily made the steep drive up Portola as the street wound its way above Eureka Valley, where Carter and I lived, and around the side of the Twin Peaks.

Marnie sighed as she looked out over the City. The day was one of those crystal clear kind. She said, "It seems like you can see forever from up here."

I grinned as we came to a stop at the intersection of Portola and O'Shaughnessy Boulevard. We were right at the bottom of the road that made its way up to the observation point on Twin Peaks. I asked, "You ever go up there to neck with any of your boyfriends?"

Marnie sat up a little straighter and replied, "I try never to talk about things like that at work."

I nodded and put the car in gear as the light changed. As we moved forward, I said, "Of course. Now, what's your plan?"

"Well, Mother's idea is that we pretend to be selling raffle tickets. I was able to buy a book at Crocker Printers over on Mission. I even tore out the first ten and wrote out fake receipts to make it look official."

I glanced over at her and smiled. "That's great, Marnie. What's the charity?"

"The Williams Beneficial Foundation." Since I was keeping my eyes on the road, I couldn't see her expression but there was a definite note of triumph in her voice.

I laughed. "You must have talked to Jeffery."

"I sure did and he's a nice fellow." She sighed. "He's also hoping I can help persuade you to read the documents he wants you to sign. But I told him you're a lost cause. I wasn't surprised to hear that you just sign anything he puts in front of you."

I shrugged. "He knows what he's doing."

"You're awfully lucky, Nick. When I told Mother—"

"Wait." I slowed down and pulled the car over to the curb. We were still a couple of blocks away, but I needed to make sure Marnie knew where I stood on things. I put on the parking brake and turned to look at her. "If you don't want me to talk about your boyfriends, I understand. It's none of my business, anyhow. But you can't talk to your mother about what I do. At least, not the specifics. It ain't ethical."

She nodded and looked down at the floorboard. "You're right, Nick. I'm sorry. I won't do it again."

"It's OK, doll." The word just slipped out before I realized I was saying it. I knew some gals didn't like words like that, so I usually tried to mind my p's and q's and not get overly familiar.

To my surprise, she looked over at me and grinned. "Doll? Sounds like a Raymond Chandler book."

I shrugged. "It kinda slipped out."

"It's OK with me. Makes me feel like we're finally doing something."

I laughed and said, "We are. Now, how do we play this?"

Chapter 6

1406 Portola Avenue
Tuesday, February 13, 1951
Just past 5 in the evening

"Yes?" An older woman opened the front door. That was the second surprise. The first had been that, although I knew where the house was, I hadn't put two and two together. That stretch of Portola was lined with nice houses built in the 20s. They were designed for well-to-do, but not rich, families with a large number of kids and a couple of servants. I knew how much Carter was taking home in his pay envelope every week and there was no way the Kellermans were able to afford to live in that kind of neighborhood.

However, the woman who answered the door appeared well off and about 60, tops. I suddenly realized she might have been his or her mother and maybe it was her house they were living in. If she was his mother-in-law, that might explain some of the tension. It would also blow Marnie's initial plan to smithereens.

In the second or two that followed, I realized Marnie was switching gears. She must have put things together like I had. She cleared her throat and said, "We're sorry to bother you, Madame, but could we have a few moments of your time to talk about aiding the victims of childhood polio?"

Suddenly, Marnie sounded polished. I tried not to laugh. I figured she was copying a voice she'd heard off the radio or in a movie. It was good.

The woman looked from Marnie to me and back. "Who, may I ask, do you represent?"

Marnie turned to me. "This is Mr. Nicholas Williams of the Williams Beneficial Foundation. I'm sure you've heard of the excellent work they're doing for the community. My name is Miss Marnie Wilson, his assistant. May we come in? We won't take but a moment of your time."

The woman blinked twice and then backed up to let us in. Once we were inside, she asked, "Won't you have a seat? May I offer you some coffee?"

Marnie said, "No, thank you. We don't want to take up too much of your time this afternoon." She paused and then asked, "May I call you Mrs. Kellerman?"

The woman nodded. "Of course."

That was a good call on Marnie's part. I thought I heard her sigh, but she remained completely composed. Everything was moving right along, which was good. But I began to notice a knot forming in my stomach. I wondered what that meant.

Marnie continued, "Mr. Williams is calling upon a select number of leading San Francisco citizens, such as yourself, to help us provide funding for polio research and to help pay for braces, iron lungs, and other much-needed supplies in the war on polio. Our contributors will be mentioned in a full-page ad in all the local papers and each one will be sent a bronze plaque, commemorating their generosity."

I tried not to let my eyes bug out too much. I could do all that, but we were way off-script and I hoped that Marnie would tone things down a bit.

Mrs. Kellerman nodded. "Yes, I'd be glad to contribute. How much are you asking?"

Before Marnie could answered, I decided to jump in. "Any amount will be helpful, Mrs. Kellerman. However, we're only able to offer recognition to donors who are willing to contribute at least one thousand dollars." I figured that might be too rich for her blood.

Out of the corner of my eye, I could see Marnie bug out for a quick moment before regaining her composure. I'd been using what Carter liked to call my "high-hat voice." It was how I'd been taught to speak in prep school. I was pretty sure Marnie hadn't heard me talk like that before.

"That'll be just fine," replied Mrs. Kellerman. "Give me a moment to write you a check. I'll be right back." She turned and opened a door not far from where she'd been standing. She switched on a light. I could briefly see an antique desk on the far side of the room. She then closed the door, leaving us alone by the front door.

Marnie looked around. "She has such a lovely home, don't you think?"

I nodded, trying very hard not to laugh. When she realized what I was doing, Marnie turned away from me and began to closely inspect the wall. I was pretty sure I heard her suppress a giggle, but I wasn't sure.

After a couple of minutes went by, I whispered, "That was a little too easy."

Marnie turned back to look at me. She was about to say something when Mrs. Kellerman exited the office with a folded-over check in her hand. Offering it to Marnie, who quickly slipped it into her pocketbook, Mrs. Kellerman turned to me and held out her hand. As we shook, she said, "It's a pleasure to finally meet you, Mr. Williams. My father, Robert Steele, was a friend and business associate of your grandfather, Michael Williams. And my dear friend, Mrs. Joanna Adams, just joined the board of your foundation. She'll be so pleased to know we've met."

I smiled and nodded. "It's definitely a pleasure to meet you, as well, but will you do me a small favor, Mrs. Kellerman?"

She nodded with a smile. "Of course."

"Please don't tell Mrs. Adams about our visit here today. I want to bring this new project to the board on my own."

Marnie added, with a laugh, "Mr. Williams is always hatching these little projects that the board isn't *always* aware of."

Mrs. Kellerman laughed. "But I'm sure they're *always* quite happy to cash the checks."

Marnie and I laughed suitably in reply. I let two beats go by before I seized an obvious opening. When she'd mentioned my grandfather's name, I'd had an idea. "Tell me, Mrs. Kellerman, what is your son's name? I seem to remember a Kellerman at St. Ignatius." That had been the prep school I'd attended, until I'd dropped out. And that wasn't a lie. There had been a Clifford Kellerman a grade or two ahead of me.

She frowned slightly and shook her head. "That would have been Cliff. He's my nephew by my late husband. My son's name is Anthony. He went to Lowell. You probably never met." Lowell was the public high school on Hayes Street, near Masonic. I wondered about that.

I nodded. "I'm sure that is much to my disadvantage."

She smiled, but it was obviously fake. "I only wish my husband had sent Anthony to St. Ignatius."

"What does your son do?" asked Marnie.

"He's a fireman." The tone of her voice made it clear she did not approve.

Marnie, taking the tack that almost every native-born San Franciscan takes on the subject of the Fire Department, enthusiastically said, "Oh, you must be so proud! Where would we be without our brave firemen?"

"Yes, of course." Mrs. Kellerman's disposition soured. I had heard that phrase—"*her disposition soured*"—before but had never seen it acted out until that moment. She then turned to me and said, "Will you excuse me? My daughter-in-law is under the weather and I need to run a quick errand to help out for dinner." She blinked a couple of times. "The cook has the night off for an early Valentine's Day and I'm left to fend for the two of us." With a deprecating giggle, she added, "I'm helpless in the kitchen."

Marnie looked over at me and then back at Mrs. Kellerman. "Won't you allow Mr. Williams to take us all out to dinner?"

I immediately piped up. "Yes, please. Since we're practically related, it would be my pleasure."

Mrs. Kellerman stepped back, obviously astonished. "I really couldn't—"

I stepped forward half a step. "Of course you can. It really would be my pleasure. Miss Wilson and myself were already talking about a place on Columbus we both enjoy." I started kicking myself mentally as soon as I said that. The place I was thinking about was a spot where Carter and I had been to on dates a few times. It was also a real hole-in-the-wall kind of joint. The waiter and the cook, his mother, would have immediately recognized me and asked about Carter.

Marnie saw Mrs. Kellerman's face fall as soon as I mentioned Columbus Avenue. She looked over at me and asked, "But I thought you had reservations for dinner at the Top of the Mark, Mr. Williams?"

Chapter 7

The Top of the Mark
999 California Street
Tuesday, February 13, 1951
A quarter past 7 in the evening

"Now, how did we get here again?" That was me and it was the third time I'd asked the question. We were standing by the bar and both drinking martinis. We'd driven ahead, at Mrs. Kellerman's request. She'd said they would call a cab.

Marnie giggled. "I still can't get over how you sound when you talk like that."

"*You* can't? What about *me*?" I asked with a grin. "It was all I could do to keep from laughing. Where'd you get all that from?"

"I was thinking about that snooty Mrs. Uppington on *Fibber McGee and Molly*, but I tried to tone it down."

I laughed. "You were good." I took a sip of my drink and asked, "Now, what do we do next?"

"Like I said, you should get Georgia, the wife, to dance with you. I'll think of things to talk about with Mrs. Kellerman. You'll have to dance with her at least once, you know."

I nodded. "Anything for Carter."

She smiled. "Yeah. Don't forget. This is your Valentine's Day gift for him." She looked at me for a long moment. "But, seriously, Nick, I have a terrible feeling about Georgia."

I nodded. I'd had a knot in my stomach since we'd walked into that house on Portola. And it hadn't gone away. "Yeah, doll. Me too."

. . .

"Mr. Williams, may I introduce, Georgia, my daughter-in-law?"

I gave her the biggest smile I could muster and shook the gal's outstretched hand. She was attractive but not pretty. She was wearing very heavy makeup, but it couldn't really hide the bruises under her left eye and along the left side of her face. While her mother-in-law was wearing an expensive dress cut in the latest style, Georgia's outfit was dowdy. That was the best word for it.

I said, "It's such a pleasure to meet you, Georgia." I didn't even bother to call her by her last name or ask her permission to use her first. It felt like using her married last name was an insult she didn't deserve. I knew I would have to keep my face focused on hers. I would never hit a lady, but that didn't mean I wasn't tempted when it came to her mother-in-law.

Right then, Marcel, the maitre d', approached. "Mr. Williams? Your table is ready."

We followed him to a table in the window. I'd slipped him a fifty to guarantee that spot. Mrs. Kellerman and

Georgia sat on one side with Georgia by the window. Marnie and I sat on the opposite side with me across from Georgia. It really was one of the best views in town but all I could focus on was Georgia and getting her out of that house.

As we looked at the menu, I heard Georgia whisper, "Oh, Mother, I just couldn't..."

I figured that was about the prices, so I turned to Marnie and asked, "What was it you had last time with Mrs. Snell?"

Marnie frowned slightly and then said, "Why, it was the Lobster Thermidor. I just adored it." It was the most expensive dish on the menu, coming in at just under eight bucks.

I looked at Georgia. "I had the same. It was delicious. Why not try it?"

Her eyes widened. "What is it?"

Mrs. Kellerman intervened and archly said, "What it is, Georgia dear, is entirely too rich for your constitution. I would recommend the cream of asparagus soup and an omelet. Much better on your stomach, my dear."

Georgia nodded meekly. "Yes, Mother."

. . .

Once dinner was ordered, I stood and asked Georgia, "May I have this dance?"

Her eyes widened in surprise, but I could see that she wanted to do so.

Mrs. Kellerman said, "Georgia, please don't overdo things."

I smiled. "We'll sneak away to the side of the dance floor, Mrs. Kellerman, I promise."

Georgia hesitated so Marnie piped up. "Oh, Nick—" She coughed. "Mr. Williams, I mean. He's a wonderful dancer. And very gentle."

I walked around to the other side of the table and made a motion to pull out Georgia's chair.

She hesitated, but then said, "Well, I guess. Just one dance."

Mrs. Kellerman sniffed and shifted in her seat. As Georgia stood, I heard Marnie ask, "Now, Mrs. Kellerman, I'm fascinated to know that your father was friends with Michael Williams. Do you happen to know how they met?"

. . .

We were dancing to an instrumental version of "Buttons and Bows." I held her close enough to be comfortable but not too close. I was worried she might have bruised ribs or something else that her dress was hiding. After thinking about it, I pulled her in just a little tighter, using my left arm to support her back. I hoped that would help her when she heard what I had to say. "Georgia, does Tony beat you often?"

She gasped and reflexively tried to pull away.

I held her tight and continued, "We're here to help you get away, if you want." I could feel her breath catch a couple of times as the tears started falling. I turned so that Mrs. Kellerman wouldn't be able to see her. I pulled her in just a little closer. "You can rest your head on my shoulder, if you want. I'm completely safe."

Finally, she said, "Yes, I think you are."

"Where do you want to go?"

"The ladies' room."

I chuckled. "In a moment. How about Los Angeles? Or back east? I'll pay for you to get to wherever you want to go. And give you some cash to get things set up when you get there. There's no reason you have to be home when Tony gets off his shift on Thursday afternoon."

She was silent for a moment. "How do you know about his shift?"

"I have a friend who works with him."

"I *hate* firemen."

"I understand. But they're not all like Tony. In fact, I think some of the other firemen have tried to get him to lay off you."

"They can all go jump in the lake, as far as I'm concerned."

I was glad to hear the anger in her voice. That was good. It meant she wanted to do something.

"Where do you want to go?"

"How do I know this isn't a scam?"

I sighed. "You don't. And I can't prove that I'm on the up-and-up."

She didn't reply to that. After a few seconds, she said, "I've always wanted to go to Seattle. I don't know why. But I even dream about it."

"Then you can go to Seattle. You can leave tomorrow morning."

"I can't." Her voice was trembling.

"What do you mean?"

"I can't leave. She won't let me."

"Your mother-in-law?"

"Yes."

"Is there any time when she's not around the house?"

"Every now and then. But she has her bridge group tomorrow. They'll be there at half past 11 and I have to clean the house in the morning."

As the song changed to "How Long Has This Been Going On?" I thought for a moment. Taking a deep breath, I asked, "Do you have to go home?"

She made an odd sort of crying sound. "What home? That house is a prison, Mr. Williams."

"Are there any papers you might need?"

"I have my driver's license with me."

"What about a birth certificate?"

"Tony keeps everything like that locked up in a strong box in the office."

I suddenly realized Mrs. Kellerman was looking at me. I smiled and let Georgia go. Leaning down, I said, "Go to the ladies' room and stay there until someone comes to get you. Do what they tell you to do. OK?"

She nodded and began to cough.

In the distance, I could see Mrs. Kellerman make a face.

"Are you faking?" I asked.

"Yes," was Georgia's reply.

I put my arm around her and walked her off the dance floor towards the ladies' room. Once we were just outside the door, I said, "Don't go anywhere until one of the staff comes to get you. OK?"

She nodded. She put her hand on the door and then hesitated.

"What?" I asked.

Looking up at me, with tears in her eyes, she asked, "Why are you doing this?"

"Because I can and because you deserve much better than what you've been getting. Now, go on in."

She gave me a faint smile and walked through the door.

. . .

I had my back to the dining room as I walked up to Marcel.

He smiled and asked, "May I help you, Mr. Williams?"

I pushed a folded-over hundred into his hand and said, "Yes. There's a lady in the ladies' room who I need to get out of the restaurant without anyone else seeing."

He narrowed his eyes for a moment.

I shook my head. "You know it's not like that. Remember Mr. Jones? The tall one?"

He shrugged. "Of course, Mr. Williams. May I ask what might be the matter?"

"It's a matter of life and death. Her husband may try to kill her." She hadn't said that, but I figured that, once he got wind of what was going on, he just might.

He looked around. "I did not see another man in your party."

"He's not here but he may be here at any moment." It was a lie, but I didn't know how else to move things along.

He nodded. "I see." He thought for a moment. "Does it matter if she leaves by the back exit?"

"That would be best."

"Yes. I will arrange it."

I smiled. "Thanks, Marcel. Have someone get her down there as quick as possible. I'll arrange for a friend to pick her up in the alley. Her name is Georgia. I told her not to go anywhere until someone from the restaurant came to get her."

He nodded again. "Be assured, Mr. Williams. We will take very good care of *Madame* Georgia."

. . .

"Hello?"

"Mike, it's Nick." I was in one of the phone booths down the hall from the restrooms. Mike Robertson was my first lover and a police lieutenant at the North Station.

"Hiya, Nick. What's up?"

"I need a huge and very unofficial favor from you."

He sighed. "What is it this time?"

"I'm at the Top of the Mark and—"

"I thought Carter was on his shift tonight."

"He is. There's a lady here and—"

"A lady?" He sounded amused.

"Mike, shut the hell up and listen, will you?"

"Sorry, Nick." He sounded annoyed.

"Look, there's a lady here who's been beaten by her husband for years and I want to get her someplace safe." She hadn't told me that directly, but I was more than sure it was true.

"You know the law about that, Nick."

"I don't give a good goddam about the law. This is an unofficial favor."

He didn't reply for a moment.

"You there?" I asked.

"Yeah. I'm trying to decide if it's worth it."

"He's a monster. I'm sure he's gonna kill her one of these days."

He sighed. "Fine. What do you want me to do?"

"Call Janet and then get over here." Janet was my sister. We weren't really close, but I knew this was something she would definitely want to help with. It was right up her alley.

"She still live—?"

"Yeah. Same place, same phone number. Tell her what I told you. She'll go with you. Then get Georgia, that's her name, somewhere safe. I'm going to put her on a plane to Seattle tomorrow."

"Now you're crossing state lines."

"I know. Are you in or not?"

He sighed again. "Fine. I'll call Janet." He paused for a moment. "Wait."

"What?"

"Why can't you call Janet?"

"I've been gone from the table too long as it is. The gal's name is Georgia. She'll be waiting by the back door in the alley. You know where that is?"

"Sure." He took a deep breath. "Why are you doing this?"

"Because she deserves a new life and a fighting chance."

"No, you have another motive. I can hear it in your voice. What is it?"

I sighed. "It's my Valentine's Day gift to Carter, if you have to know."

He was silent for a moment.

"I gotta go, Mike."

"I know." His voice was a lot softer than before. "I'll take care of it. Don't worry, Nick."

Before I could reply, the line went dead.

. . .

"I'm so sorry, Mrs. Kellerman, I had to—"

"What I'd like to know, Mr. Williams, is where is Georgia?" Her voice was arch, and her tone was piercing. The woman at the table behind her looked at me in surprise while her male companion narrowed his eyes in my direction.

The waiter had just delivered our meal. Marnie had somehow managed to keep Mrs. Kellerman at the table while I'd been talking to Marcel and was then on the phone with Mike. I replied, "She wasn't feeling well and wanted an aspirin. I suggested that she ask the attendant for one."

Mrs. Kellerman rose. I stood as she did. "Mr. Williams, will you excuse me? Georgia is a frail woman. Anthony expects me to keep an eye on her." With that, she threw her napkin on the table and stormed around the dance floor and towards the ladies' room.

Marnie said, "Nick!"

I nodded. "I know, doll." I quickly explained what I'd been up to.

She took it in and then asked, "What if Georgia is still in there when the battle-axe barges in?"

I asked, "Could you—?"

She was gone before I could finish speaking.

. . .

I sat at the table, alone, and kept my eye on the ladies' room door. After about five minutes, I saw Mrs. Kellerman storm out with Marnie in tow. The two of them made a beeline to the table, crossing the dance floor in spite of the couples dancing as the band played a lively version of "The Third Man Theme."

When Mrs. Kellerman arrived at the table, I stood. She was red in the face. "I demand you do something!"

I leaned forward. "What's happened?"

"Georgia left by the employee exit!"

I nodded and folded my arms. After pretending to think it over, I said, "You two have a seat and begin dinner. I'll go find her. Don't worry."

Mrs. Kellerman stared at me for a long moment, as if she wasn't buying what I was selling. Finally, she sighed. "Fine. I'm glad there's a man on hand to take care of her. She's more than a handful and Anthony does expect a lot from me."

I walked around and pulled out her chair so she could sit. I then scooted around the table and did the same for Marnie. "You ladies get started and I'm sure Georgia and I will be back before you know it."

. . .

"Thanks." I handed the bellman a folded-over ten. Marcel had arranged for him to take me down to the lobby and then through a maze of stairs and hallways until we got to the back door. If it hadn't been for him, I would have gotten lost trying to make it through the building on my own.

I pushed open the door and found Georgia standing next to my sister, Janet. Mike was in his Ford and the engine was running.

Janet looked up. "Good. You're here. Can you convince her we're here to help?" She sounded more aggravated than she usually did.

I smiled at Georgia and then I put my hand on Janet's arm. "This is my sister. Her name is Janet."

Georgia relaxed. "Thanks, Mr. Williams." Looking at Janet, she added, "I'm sorry. I've never done this before and it's so confusing."

Mike called out through the open passenger-door window, "We need to get out of here. Now."

I said, "And that's Mike. He's one of my best friends. He's kinda scary looking but he's a real pussycat."

Georgia giggled a little and then asked, "Where am I going?"

Janet crossed her arms. "Yeah, where are we going?" For the first time, I noticed Janet had cut her hair since I'd seen her last. She looked good, even in the dim light of the alley.

I pushed a couple of twenties into her hand and said, "Take her down to some motel near the airport. Check in under your name and stay with her tonight, if you don't mind. Call the office and tell the service where you are once you get there. I'll get there as soon as I can. And I'll arrange for her to be on the first flight to Seattle tomorrow morning."

She nodded and opened the back door of Mike's car. "You can sit in here, Georgia."

The woman meekly got in. Janet closed the door behind her. Turning back to me, she asked, "What is this about?"

"Have a good look at her face when you get a chance." I leaned in and whispered, "This is for all those men on the street who needed a buck."

She sighed and nodded, pursing her lips tightly as she did.

I reached out and hugged her. As usual, she let me but was stiff in my arms.

. . .

"Mr. Williams! This is unacceptable!"

I was standing with Marnie and Mrs. Kellerman just outside the restrooms. She was pink with indignation.

"I'm so sorry, Mrs. Kellerman. She's left the hotel. One of the hotel staff saw her catch a cab and then she was gone."

The woman shook her head and looked at me. "Why do I think you have something to do with this? Who were you calling?"

I decided the best response was indignation. "I'm not sure what you're implying, Mrs. Kellerman. I was on the telephone with a business associate."

"And why were you talking for such a long time with that ridiculous maitre d'?"

I frowned slightly. "He was asking me about a private matter."

Marnie asked, "Was that in regards to the foundation, Mr. Williams?"

I crossed my arms and tried to glare at Marnie. "As you well know, Miss Wilson, we never discuss such matters in public."

She looked down, doing a good job of appearing to be abashed. "Of course," she whispered.

Mrs. Kellerman looked around. "Well, what am I to do? My Anthony is at that loathsome firehouse and now Georgia is missing."

I sighed. "My suggestion would be to return home where I'm sure you will find her."

"And if she's not there?"

"Then file a missing person's report with the police."

She went pale, which surprised me. "The police?" Her voice was suddenly quiet and meek.

"Of course. That's the proper authority."

She shook her head. "Oh, no, Mr. Williams. I couldn't."

Marnie walked around and put her hand on the older woman's arm. "Why don't we go downstairs and put you a cab? You can go home. I'm sure that's where Georgia must be."

Mrs. Kellerman sighed. "I suppose you're right."

On a hunch, I asked, "Has she done this before?"

The older woman nodded. "Twice. That's why I'm reluctant to contact the police." Showing a glimmer of humanity, she added, in a sad tone of voice, "She's always come back, poor thing."

Chapter 8

Driving south on Bayshore Boulevard
Tuesday, February 13, 1951
A quarter past 9 in the evening

"This unraveled a lot faster than I thought it would." That was me talking to Marnie. We'd stopped at my house so I could get some money for Georgia. We'd also called the service. Janet had left a message that they were at the E-Z Court Motel on El Camino Real in Millbrae. That was where we were headed.

"What do you mean, Nick?"

"I thought we'd probably be helping her move out tomorrow morning and then taking her down to the airport after that."

"That's what I thought, too. What happened?"

"She said that Mrs. Kellerman has a bridge party tomorrow and that she, meaning Georgia, has to clean the house in the morning. It sounds like she's a prisoner in that place."

Marnie nodded. "You should have heard the old lady. The whole time you were dancing with Georgia, she was complaining about how lazy she was and didn't pull her weight. It was awful."

I nodded as we crossed into San Mateo County and continued south.

"I'm real glad we're doing this, Nick. I can't imagine leaving her in that place one more minute."

"Yeah, doll. And it was all your idea. If you hadn't asked me about doing something *for* Carter, I wouldn't have thought about it."

She giggled. "Oh, I doubt that."

Neither of us talked for a moment. Finally, she said, "I like working with you, Nick. I'm real sorry for Georgia, but this is what I was hoping we'd end up doing, at some point."

I laughed. "Well, doll, it's like I told you when I hired you, doing P.I. stuff is usually boring. But, every now and then, something like this comes along. Just don't count on it happening very often." I turned and looked at her in the dim light of the dashboard. "Thanks for being the brains of the operation, doll. You think fast on your feet."

She giggled. "Oh, Nick."

. . .

"How is she?" Mike, Janet, Marnie, and I were in Room 7. Georgia was resting in Room 9.

Janet said, "She's scared. I don't think she trusts us. I can't blame her." She looked at me. "How did you get involved in this?"

I shrugged. "Carter works with her husband. He was telling me today about how the guy beats her."

Marnie piped up. "This is Nick's Valentine's Day gift for Carter."

I held my breath. I didn't want to tell Janet that. She was a lot more cynical than me and she tended to believe that people should take care of themselves and mind their own business. She was more like our father than not, in that sense.

She crossed her arms. "That so?"

I nodded. "Yeah."

Mike, sensing trouble, said, "It doesn't matter why Nick is doing this. Someone needed to help this poor woman. The reason may be loony but it's a good thing as far as I'm concerned."

Janet turned on him. "Isn't this illegal?"

Mike nodded. "Sure."

She pressed him. "And you're OK with that?"

"Just because the law treats a married woman like a piece of property doesn't mean she is one." He was sounding a little heated.

Janet looked down at the little rug on the motel room floor. "I guess you're right."

"Do you mind spending the night here?" I was looking at Janet when I asked that.

Before she could answer, Marnie piped up. "I'm going to take care of that." Without waiting for me to agree or disagree, she stood and continued, "I'm going to call Mother and let her know I'll be here for the night." With that, she opened the door and was gone.

Janet looked at me. "Where'd you find her?"

I shrugged. "She's a good hire."

Mike grinned at me. "I had no idea she was that smart. Your girl, Georgia, gave us a blow-by-blow of how this all came together. Doesn't sound like your kind of plan, Nick."

I shook my head and grinned. "It wasn't. Marnie came up with the whole thing and was fast on her feet. She's a lot smarter than I would have guessed."

Mike folded his arms. "Does this mean you're going to take some real cases from now on?"

I shrugged. "We'll see."

Janet leaned over and put her hand on my arm. "I'm proud of you, big brother."

I smiled. "Thanks, sis."

. . .

Once Marnie was back, I said, "Next thing is to get her a ticket on the first flight to Seattle tomorrow morning."

Mike looked at his watch. "It's nearly 10:30. That'll have to wait until the morning."

Marnie said, "It's United flight 671. It departs at 9:10 a.m and arrives in Seattle at 12:10 p.m. And I'm going with her."

Mike and I both shook our heads. I said, "No. You could get in a lot of trouble under the Mann Act." That was the federal law that was supposed to protect women from white slavery but usually kept them tied to their no-good husbands.

Marnie nodded and smoothed out her dress. "I understand. But we can't let that woman go up there all alone."

Mike said, "Marnie, I don't think you understand. Helping her leave her husband could be considered an 'immoral purpose' and, if Kellerman decides to call the F.B.I., you're looking at up to five years."

She nodded. "I understand. So does Mother. She's coming too."

"No," I said. "This is serious business, Marnie."

She shrugged. "I don't care." Squaring her shoulders, she asked, "So, are you gonna give me the money so I can get three plane tickets in the morning or not?" She held out her hand.

I sighed. "Marnie, I could—"

Janet said, "Four tickets."

I frowned. "What?"

"You heard me. We'll make it a girl's trip." She grinned at Marnie who nodded.

Mike said, "You two are treading very thin ice. I should arrest you both right now."

Marnie held out her wrists. "Fine, Mr. Robertson. Slap 'em on me."

Janet did the same and added, "Then you can cuff me."

Mike looked at me.

I shrugged and pulled out my wallet.

Chapter 9

The Top of the Mark
999 California Street
Thursday, February 15, 1951
Half past 7 in the evening

As we sat across from each other, I held up my martini glass and he lifted his beer glass. We clinked and I said, "Happy late Valentine's Day, Carter."

He smiled as we both took a drink. He asked, "What'd you do the last couple of days?" It was the first chance we'd had to talk since he'd gotten home from the firehouse about half past 4. I'd given him a bath and then we'd fooled around in bed, necking mostly, until it was time to get ready for dinner. In all that time, we hadn't talked much. We usually didn't in the first couple of hours after he got off his shift.

I shook my head. "Nope. You first."

He shrugged. "Well, the first sixteen hours were quiet. Then all hell broke loose around 8 yesterday morning."

Right then, the waiter walked up to ask about our orders. Carter put in for a porterhouse steak, well-done, and I decided to have the Lobster Thermidor.

Once the man was gone, Carter asked, "You've never had that before. What gives?"

I shrugged. "It's kind of a special dish."

He frowned. "Really?"

I nodded. "Yeah."

He smiled. "Fine. So, where was I?"

"All hell had just broken loose."

He nodded. "Yes. So, remember me telling you about Kellerman?"

"I think so."

"Seems like his wife left him."

"Really?"

Carter nodded and took a sip of his beer. "I didn't get the whole story but, apparently, she and his mother went out to dinner with some hotshot and, in the middle of everything, she left through the service entrance and was gone."

I managed to keep a straight face and asked, "How'd he take it?"

"The first thing he did was to pull the phone off the wall and then he smashed it."

"With his fist?"

"Nope. With a fire axe."

I sat back. "What an animal."

"That ain't the worst of it, son. He went after the captain."

"With the axe?"

Carter nodded. "It was something else. The captain tried to calm him down and Kellerman went after him with the blunt end. Nearly knocked the captain out but he was too fast for Kellerman and a couple of the other guys—Carlo was one of 'em—got him down on the ground. The captain called dispatch and two cops from North Station showed up, followed by Mike, of all people."

"That so?"

"Yes. They took him away and he's in lock-up as far as I know. This morning, Captain said the District Attorney was trying to decide whether to charge him with attempted murder or send him away somewhere for treatment. Seems like Kellerman might be nuts."

"Sounds like it. Did Mike stay cool when he saw you?"

Carter nodded. "I got the impression he stepped in to take the call when it went out because he knew it was Station Three."

"Probably."

Carter took a sip of his beer. "We had a couple of cats up in trees but nothing much until this morning, when we got called in on a four-alarm fire around 9."

"Where was it?"

"Another one of those big wooden houses in the Western Addition. It was on McAllister near Laguna. The neighbors said it was abandoned. From what I could tell, it was probably electrical. I didn't get a whiff of any sort of gasoline or anything like that. Captain and I are gonna go over it tomorrow afternoon." Carter had a very sensitive nose and he worked a lot on arson investigations.

We both took a drink. He looked at me. "So, what about you?"

"Well, a few things happened while you were gone."

"Really?"

"First off, I didn't get to tell you, but lunch on Tuesday was wonderful. Thank you."

He grinned. "You're welcome, Nick."

"I took Jeffery to the Old Poodle Dog for dinner last night. Or I was going to."

Carter asked, "Where was Adam in all this?"

"I'm getting to that. So, when I saw Jeffery on Tuesday, before our lunch, he told me he was only with Adam because he didn't wanna be alone on Valentine's Day. I told him to let me take him out and to forget Adam. So, apparently, on Tuesday night, he called Adam and it didn't go very well."

"That so?"

"Yeah. So, I show up at Jeffery's house at 7 last night and Adam is there, trying to convince Jeffery to get back together."

"What happened?"

I shrugged. "I gave Adam a C-note and told him to take my reservation at the restaurant and to be good to Jeffery. Then I went to the Alhambra and saw *Dallas* with Gary Cooper. It was OK."

Carter finished off his beer and asked, "So what else happened?"

I reached into my coat for my wallet, opened it, and pulled out a folded-over piece of paper. I handed it to Carter and said, "Happy Valentine's Day."

He took the paper, smiled, and read it. He then looked up with a frown. "A receipt for four plane tickets on United Airlines to Seattle? What does this mean? Are we going to Seattle?"

I shook my head. "No. This is my gift to you. I did something for you. And it was Marnie's suggestion. Turns out, she's a helluva smart gal."

Carter said, "I still don't get it."

"I know. I'm gonna explain it."

Carter sat back.

Right then, the waiter walked up. "Another Burgermeister, sir?"

Carter nodded. "Thanks."

The waiter then looked at me. "A fresh martini?"

I shook my head. "I'm fine for now. Maybe after the food comes."

He nodded. "Very good. I'll be right back with your beer." With that, he walked off.

Carter crossed his arms. "OK. What happened?"

"Tuesday morning, while you were preparing lunch, I asked Marnie to help me figure out what to get you."

"You waited until the 13th?"

I shrugged. "I worried about it for a month and then I asked Marnie. I had a crazy idea about arranging for a flower delivery van to crash in front of the firehouse so that flowers would be scattered everywhere, but that didn't seem practical."

Carter gave me half a smile. "No, but I like the thought."

"So, I asked Marnie and she suggested I do something *for* you instead of just buying something. Like you did."

"Uh huh."

"When she said that, a light bulb went off. I remembered you telling me about Kellerman."

Carter's eyes narrowed. "Kellerman?"

I nodded. "Yeah. So, I told her about the guy and what he was doing to his wife."

"You did?"

I looked over at Carter. His emerald-green eyes were flashing. I held up my right hand. "Before you—"

He leaned forward. "Are you the big shot that his mother and wife were out with on Tuesday night?"

I nodded.

He stared for a moment. Then he blinked a couple of times. Right then, the waiter arrived with a new beer.

Looking up at the man, I said, "I'll take that martini, after all."

Nodding, the waiter walked off.

Carter took a long drink, draining half his glass.

When he was done, he carefully put his beer down and looked at me. "What exactly did you do?"

"Well, Marnie had a great idea. We drove over to their house—"

Carter's eyes widened. "You went to Kellerman's house?"

I nodded. "Yeah. It's one of those nice jobs from the 20s. Two stories. Room for a maid and a cook."

Carter frowned. "A maid and a cook?"

"Yeah. And they have a cook. And Georgia was the maid."

He frowned again. "Georgia?" Then he nodded thoughtfully. "Oh, right. His wife."

"She looked awful. And she couldn't wait to leave."

Carter sat back. "So you and Marnie took Georgia and Mrs. Kellerman out to dinner?"

"Yeah. We brought her here, as a matter of fact."

He cocked his head. "That so?"

"Yeah. And I asked her to dance, Georgia that is. I told her she could go anywhere. She decided on Seattle. So, I stashed her in the ladies' room and—"

"You did what?"

"Mrs. Kellerman was watching us. After hearing Georgia talk about her home life, I realized she had to leave right then. So, I stashed her in the ladies' room. Then I got Marcel to have someone take her down to the back door. I called Mike. He got Janet—"

Carter held up his hand. "Wait. So, Mike and Janet were in on this?"

I nodded. Right then the waiter arrived with my martini. I took it from him and immediately had a long drink from the glass. I was beginning to worry that things weren't going to turn out like I'd hoped.

Carter watched me. As he did, his features softened. Leaning forward, he said, "I'm not mad at you, Nick."

I sighed. "Maybe I shouldn't have done what I did."

He sat back in his seat and looked at me for a long moment. Finally, he sighed and said, "Go on."

I pulled out a pack of Camels and lit one with my beat-up old Zippo. After taking a long drag, I said, "Well, Mike went and picked up Janet." I began to fiddle with the ashtray, keeping my eyes on the table. "They met us down in the alley and then took Georgia to a motel in Millbrae. Then Mike lectured them about the Mann Act." I looked up. Carter was smiling. "What?" I asked.

He shook his head. "Nothing. Just thinking about good ole Lieutenant Mike. What else?"

I shrugged. "That was it. Marnie arranged everything. She and her mother and Janet left for Seattle with Georgia at 9 yesterday morning. I heard from Marnie this morning. They're getting Georgia settled in and the three of them will be back tomorrow afternoon."

Carter, who was looking amused, asked, "And I suppose you're footing the bill for all of this?"

I nodded. "Sure."

"Well, it sounds like quite an adventure."

"Yeah."

His smile broke into a full grin. "Maybe someday you'll do more of that kind of work instead of just following all those wayward husbands and wives around."

I took a sip of my martini. "Maybe." I paused for a moment and then added. "You shoulda seen Marnie. She was something else."

He nodded. "Sounds like you were something else, yourself."

"So, was it OK what I did?" I usually never asked a question like that, but I needed to know.

He thought for a moment and then picked up his

glass of beer. He drained it, put it down, wiped his mouth with the back of his hand, and stood.

"What?" I asked, looking up at him.

He buttoned his coat and, with a big grin, said, "Come on, son. I can't wait for us to eat dinner. I want you all to myself. Right now. Let's go home."

I stood, dropped a fifty on the table, and followed the man I loved to the elevator as the band played our song, "Some Enchanted Evening." They were right. It certainly was.

Washington's Birthday
1948

Preface

This is the story of what happens one night over dinner at Gene Compton's Cafeteria at Market and Van Ness in San Francisco.

There's no plot, no surprise reveal, and not much happens other than we get to know more about Nick Williams and his good friend, Kenneth "Mack" McKnight, during the first few months of Nick's long relationship with Carter Jones. For his part, Carter is not found in this story since he's busy protecting the good citizens of 1948 San Francisco as a fireman on duty that night at Station 3 over on Post Street.

As might have happened in any of the many cafeterias in the City in those days, a couple of friends will likely drop by for a chat.

But there won't be a shoot-out or any mystery to solve. This is just a snippet of time in a world that is long gone, but not forgotten.

I hope you enjoy the tale!

The Story

Gene Compton's Cafeteria
Market and Van Ness
San Francisco, Cal.
Monday, February 23, 1948
Half past 6 in the evening

With only a bowl of navy bean soup, a couple of slices of bread, and a cup of coffee on his tray, Nick Williams stood and surveyed the room. Off in the back corner, he spied his friend, Kenneth "Mack" McKnight, seated at a table for four. Nick headed in that direction.

On his way over, he passed by several tables of families with mostly well-behaved children, but none of the usual crowd. They wouldn't be out and about until half past 8 or later. Nick planned to be long gone by then. He wasn't much in the mood for that sort of fun and games.

Mack's head was buried in a copy of the late edition of the *Examiner*. He was just about finished eating one of the two turkey sandwiches on his tray. A cup of coffee completed his meal.

Nick was just about to put down his tray when, without looking up from his paper, Mack said, "Hey, sailor." That was his usual greeting.

Grinning, Nick sat, dropped his napkin in his lap, and picked up his spoon. "Whatcha readin' there?"

Folding over his paper and placing it to the side of his tray, Mack said, "The Arabs exploded a bomb in Jerusalem, the commies are about to take over Czechoslovakia, and, although there's flooding in Oregon, our drought has no end in sight."

"And the governor is talking about rationing electricity," said Nick as he dipped his spoon into his bowl of soup and began to swirl it around.

"Yeah," replied Mack. "So, how's your day been, sailor?"

"Boring."

"You work at the hospital overnight?"

"Yeah. Got off at 6 this morning. Took a cab home. Tried to sleep and made it until noon. Scrambled a couple of eggs and made some coffee and then headed out for a walk."

Mack grinned lecherously. "Meet anyone while you were out and about?"

Nick rolled his eyes. "How many times do I have to tell you?" He lowered his voice and leaned forward. "Carter Jones is the real deal." He was feeling hot under the collar, like he had several times in the last few months when talking about Carter with not only Mack, but a few other friends.

For his part, Mack didn't reply. He just bit into his sandwich and went back to his paper.

. . .

"What movie did you see?" ask Mack after he finished his second sandwich and folded over the *Examiner*. The two men had eaten in silence for a few minutes.

"*Albuquerque*."

"Randolph Scott and Gabby Hayes?"

"Yeah," replied Nick, still a little steamed at Mack but letting it roll off his back as much as he could.

"Whadja think?"

Nick shrugged. "It was fine. Kept me entertained." He looked up from the last of his soup. "You see it?"

"Sure," replied Mack as he shifted in his chair so he could stretch out his long legs. "Saw it yesterday." He grinned at Nick, crossed his arms, and leaned back a little. "*Ha ha ha, you and me, little brown jug, don't I love thee?*" He was quietly singing the tune from the cartoon that they showed before the movie.

In spite of himself, Nick started to grin as he reached into his coat pocket and pulled out his pack of Camels.

"But," said Mack, "those aren't the words they had under the bouncing ball on the screen."

"Oh?" asked Nick as he reached for his Zippo.

Mack nodded. "I had an uncle who used to sing it like how I just did." His eyes narrowed a little as he watched Nick light his cigarette. Leaning forward, he reached across the table and gently took the Zippo from Nick's hand. He looked at the way the thing was bent in the middle for a moment and then handed it back over. "I still remember that night you and me stuffed ourselves in that berth built for one and bent your poor old lighter."

Nick pocketed his Zippo, took a long drag, and then exhaled to his left. "Yeah. So do I."

"You miss those days?"

That was a hard question for Nick to answer. Ever since he'd met Carter and gotten to know the fireman,

Nick had begun to realize that no other man he'd been with had ever really loved him the way Carter did. Two came close, however, and Mack was one of them.

Not wanting to hurt his friend's feelings, Nick grinned a little and said, "Sure. Those were some swell days and fun nights when we were on that ship on our way home."

Mack frowned a little and crossed his arms again. "Would you be willing to come back into my bed if I was to ask you?"

Nick didn't hesitate. "No. Like I said, what's goin' on between me and Carter is the real deal."

Glancing over Nick's shoulder, Mack said, "Here comes trouble."

"Who?"

"John Templeton."

More to himself than to Mack, Nick muttered, "Doesn't he ever take 'no' for an answer?"

"Apparently not."

"Mind if I join you two?" asked John Templeton with his usual cheery demeanor that always rubbed Nick the wrong way.

"It's a free country," replied Mack with a smile that wasn't very friendly, but wasn't rude, either.

As he put his tray down and had a seat, John said, "Well, I've really had a wonderful day. How about the two of you?" His meal consisted of a chef's salad and a cup of coffee.

"Mine was OK," said Nick as he took a final drag off his cigarette and then stubbed out the remains in the glass ashtray.

"Mine, too," added Mack.

"Well, I spent my day roaming the stores around Union Square that were open, considering it's a holiday, and snatching up what I could that's on sale, and there's a lot that is, believe you me."

"Why?" asked Mack, looking a little befuddled.

"Washington's Birthday sales in the stores are the *best* time to pick up birthday presents, *and* Christmas presents." John popped a tomato wedge in his mouth and enthusiastically chewed.

"Oh," said Mack.

"Is that all you did all day?" asked Nick, immediately wishing he'd kept his mouth shut as soon as he spoke.

John nodded. "Oh, yes. And my feet are *killing* me. I just finished putting all my treasures away at home." He dug around in his bowl with his fork. "Tomorrow, or maybe Wednesday, I'll begin to wrap everything and put labels on each package."

"Sounds like a lotta work," offered Mack.

"It is, but it's so worth it." Looking at Nick, John smiled and said, "I think I even found something you might like for your birthday."

"My birthday?" asked Nick as he reached for his pack of Camels again.

"Sure. You told me your birthday is at the end of November." Pointing at Nick with his fork, John continued, "That makes you a Sagittarius and I'm convinced I found *just* the thing." He grinned and, with a teasing voice, said, "But you'll have to wait until November to find out."

By that time, Nick had lit a second cigarette. He exhaled, again, to his left.

"What'd you do today?" asked John.

"He went to see *Albuquerque*," replied Mack with a whisper of a grin on his face.

John took a drink from his coffee mug and then asked, "What'd you think of it?"

"It was fine," replied Nick.

"Well..." John wiped his mouth with his napkin. He was obviously about to settle in to tell Nick another one of his Hollywood stories. "When I was working down there, you know, during the war, everyone, but *everyone*, knew all about Randolph Scott and Cary Grant."

"What about them?" asked Mack.

Ignoring him and keeping his big hazel eyes focused on Nick, John said, "Well, for one thing, they were lovers." The way he said it made Nick think John was either jealous or lying. Nick couldn't quite figure out which might be true.

"They were?" That was Mack, again.

"In the 30s, they shared a house off Los Feliz Boulevard before moving to Santa Monica. There was even a big spread in one of the movie magazines showing them looking lovingly at each other across the breakfast table. Can you beat that?"

"No," replied Nick as he took another puff on his Camel.

"And then there was that movie."

"A blue movie?" asked Mack, sounding a little titillated.

"You know," prompted John as he kept his eyes on Nick.

"The one with Irene Dunne?" asked Nick, already tired of the conversation and hoping the floor would open up and John would be swallowed into a great big hole, never to be seen again.

"Yes! *My Favorite Wife*!"

"I loved that movie," enthused Mack.

Nick winked across the table as John said, "There's that scene, don't you know, where Cary Grant can't seem to stop thinking about Randolph Scott. I mean, isn't that just the end-all?"

"Sure," replied Nick as he stubbed out his cigarette in the ashtray.

John looked down at his salad and poked at it with his fork. He hadn't eaten much of it. He hadn't had a chance since all he'd done was talk since he sat down.

No one spoke for all of ten seconds. Then John looked at his watch. "Goodness!"

"What?" asked Mack.

"I'm so sorry, Nick, but I have to run."

"Oh?"

"Yes. I'm due for cocktails at the Pied Piper bar in the Palace." He glanced at Mack and then frowned at Nick. "I'd invite you to join us, but"—he put his hand on Nick's arm as if he was about to deliver some really bad news—"I'm afraid you probably wouldn't enjoy the crowd."

Nick shrugged. He didn't care one bit and that was the truth.

Squeezing his arm, John leaned a little closer. "When are we going to have that date I keep hoping for? It will be my treat." He tilted his head sympathetically. "I know hospital orderlies don't make that much." He then smiled as his eyes darted around Nick's face. "Even ones as cute as you with such a sweet dimple and those beautiful brown eyes."

Nick held perfectly still. He'd told John, over and over again, that he was seeing Carter Jones. What's more, he didn't like being fawned over. Particularly when the guy couldn't take a hint.

John's eyebrows began to creep up his forehead as he waited for an answer.

Finally, Nick said, "I'm really busy these days. Those bedpans won't empty themselves."

His nose wrinkling in distaste, John let go of Nick's arm and stood. "Well, maybe soon." He patted Nick's shoulder and quickly walked towards the exit, leaving his mostly uneaten salad behind along with a whiff of bay rum.

. . .

"Can I bum a Camel?" asked Mack after he'd returned from removing their collection of trays, dirty plates, and silverware and refilling both their mugs of coffee.

"Sure," said Nick. He tapped his pack against the side of his hand so that the next willing one would slide out.

Mack grabbed it with two thick fingers. Nick pocketed his cigarettes and reached for the Zippo. Once Mack was all lit up and had taken a deep drag, he exhaled above the table and grinned. "How much do you have on deposit at Bank of America as of close of business on Friday?"

Nick felt his face begin to burn as he shrugged and replied, "It's all in a trust, so I don't know, and I don't care."

Mack sucked in and blew out again. "What I don't understand is why you let everyone in the world believe you're just a Navy vet, with no discernible skills,"—Mack grinned at that—"who was barely lucky enough to find a job working as an orderly at City Hospital." He took in another drag. "As far as I know, me and Jeffery Klein are the only ones who know the truth that you're probably the richest man in San Francisco."

"Mike knows."

Mack nodded with a slight smirk. "How *is* the first love of your life, Sergeant Robertson, these days?"

"Fine, as far as I know. I haven't seen him in a couple of weeks. And he's about to be promoted to lieutenant."

Mack's smirk turned to a smile. "Really? Good for him."

Nick nodded.

"And what about your father?"

With that subject mentioned, Nick was ready for another Camel. Once lit, he contemplated the burning end and then said what he, more or less, always said, "I have no idea and I couldn't care less."

Mack leaned forward. "At some point—"

"Nope." Nick took a puff and then blew the smoke right in Mack's face. "Next topic. Or are you ready to head home?"

Easing back, Mack shrugged. "I got nowheres to be. How about you?"

"Carter doesn't get home until tomorrow morning."

Mack crossed his arms. "Are you really in love with him?"

Nick nodded as he took another drag.

"I like him," said Mack, "but he's such a hick."

Rolling his eyes, Nick hotly replied, "Carter Jones is one of the smartest people I've ever known, bar none."

Mack snorted. "But that accent."

"So?"

"And I know he didn't go to college or anything." Mack started smirking again. "Unlike your doppelganger... What's his name?"

"Henry Wilson." Nick rolled his eyes again. "And Henry is much more attractive than me."

"I guess you're right about that." Running his finger down his cheek, Mack added, "That scar makes me wanna do things to him, even though I get the feeling he's not nearly as experienced as you are."

He wasn't. Not by a long shot. Nick knew the answer because of what Carter had told him. Henry and Carter had grown up together in Georgia. They'd become lovers on their move from there to San Francisco. But that had ended when Henry left to go into the Army which was how he got the scar on his face. A German officer he was arresting didn't like that fact and had used a knife to let Henry know.

Truth be told, Nick liked Henry a lot. Probably more than Carter did, in fact. So, he wasn't about to say anything about his friend that might end up getting passed around town. Mack could sometimes be a real gossip.

"Dunno," said Nick.

"I bet there's not much you don't know about Carter and Henry. You're always good at getting people to tell you about their lives. You should be one of those private dicks, like Philip Marlowe or Sam Spade."

Before he could stop himself, Nick said, "You've still never told me anything about where you're from other than to say you grew up in Pittsburgh."

"Wanna take me home and try to get the truth outta me?"

Nick was playing with his Zippo when Mack said that. He banged it on the table and said, "When are you gonna get it through that thick skull of yours that I'm in love?" He leaned forward. "Look, Mack. When we got home and you decided you weren't ready to 'play house', I didn't say anything because we were just the kind of friends who do things together."

Mack's eyes were flashing, which was a warning signal that he was about to get up and bolt out of the cafeteria. Mack hated arguments. So he ran whenever he got angry like he was right then.

But Nick didn't care. He was itching to say what he needed to say. "But these last few months, ever since Carter and I started going together, you're all of a sudden as frisky as a colt. When I was with Jeffery, you never once said anything like that."

"You know why?"

"No. Why?"

Mack leaned forward. He was still angry, but his eyes were back to normal. He hissed, "Because he told me he would send a private dick to Pittsburgh and find out who I really was if I ever made a move on you."

That stopped Nick in his tracks. "Who you really were? What does that mean?"

"One day, back around Christmas of '45, I ran into Jeffery on the street and he started grilling me. Said he wanted to know my real name and where I'd gone to school. That sorta thing."

The idea of Jeffery talking like that to Mack, who could have easily made mincemeat of the guy, made Nick smile.

"Why are you grinning?"

"Jeffery is a real lightweight. You could have easily —"

"Save that," interrupted Mack with a dismissive wave. "I know you think I'm some big hulk of a guy who likes to fight, but I'd bet your fireman is better at that than I am."

Nick shrugged. "I have a hard time imagining Jeffery having the guts to pull a stunt like that."

"I think there's a lot about Jeffery that you don't know."

"Such as?"

Before Mack could say anything, a feminine-sounding voice behind Nick said, "Well, hello there, you two!"

Mack pointed to the chair where John Templeton had been sitting earlier. "Won't you join us?"

"Don't mind if I do."

Nick grinned at the newcomer and asked, "How've you been Suzy?"

"Just peachy, hon. Thanks for asking." She was wearing a light-gray tailored suit with a red and green scarf tied around her neck to hide her Adam's apple, something she'd told Nick about the last time he saw her which was in the very same spot about two weeks earlier.

"Hungry?" asked Mack, which was a good question since Suzy was perennially broke.

"No, but thank you. I just finished a job and it included dinner."

"Where?" asked Nick.

"The Fairmont. Afterwards, we ate in the dining room, and it was lovely." Suzy smiled in that charming way she had. "But, after so much Nob Hill stuffiness, I needed to come down here and let my hair down." She patted the back of her golden blonde wig. "Just a little bit, anyway."

"Who was your client?" asked Mack, something he always did whenever Suzy talked shop.

"Some bigwig from Salt Lake City." She made a face and then, in a whisper, said, "You wouldn't believe the bizarre clothes that man was wearing under his suit."

"Really?" asked Nick, curious.

"All sorts of things written on them and such." She waved her manicured hand. "But I paid no attention and got the job done."

In a concerned tone, Mack asked, "Was he good to you, Suzy?"

"I can take care of myself, hon." She then smiled. "But, yes, he was sweet. The out-of-towners always are." She turned to Nick. "And where is your fireman tonight? At work?"

Nodding, Nick took a sip of his coffee. "Yeah."

She put a hand on his arm. "It really is the real thing, isn't it?"

Nick nodded, suddenly missing Carter more than he had all day, which was saying a lot.

"Please tell him I said, 'hello,' won't you?"

"I will. And I'm sure he says the same. You're one of his favorite people, Suzy."

She blushed and put her hand up to her fabric-swaddled throat. "Oh, my. Well..." She was silent for a couple of beats. "That really is nice to know." Looking at Mack and then at Nick, she added, "You three really are more than kind to me. I'm always happy to see you when I do, and I know..." She teared up right then.

Nick reached into his pocket, pulled out his handkerchief, and offered it.

Taking it, Suzy dabbed her eyes and then handed it back. "Thanks, Nick."

"You're welcome."

She sniffed and then said, "Well, I guess I need to get home."

"How are you set for a cab?" asked Mack.

Waving him away with a grateful smile, Suzy replied, "Oh, you're more than sweet, hon. But Mr. Young was very generous, and I'm good for a while." She quietly added, "After I pay my back rent and such."

"I worry about you, Suzy," said Mack, obviously meaning it.

"And I worry about *you*," was her frank reply.

"You do?" asked Nick.

Mack blushed as Suzy said, "He still talks in sleep when he *does* sleep, and I worry about that. Don't you?" She knew all about their history, but Nick had no idea Mack and Suzy had spent *that* kind of time together.

Before Nick could reply, Mack got up and pulled out Suzy's chair so she could stand. Nick pushed back his chair, rose, and gave Suzy a kiss on the cheek.

She blushed and touched her face where he'd kissed her. "Oh, my, Mr. Williams. You always take my breath away."

He smiled. "Take care of yourself, Suzy."

She straightened her coat, adjusted her hat, and smoothed out her skirt. "I always do."

Towering above her slender frame, Mack offered his arm. "May I walk with you outside?"

She blushed again and nodded.

Nick smiled to himself as he watched the two make their way through the maze of tables.

...

It was Nick's turn to get refills on coffee, so he did just that. As he stood at one of the big urns and filled the two mugs, he glanced across the room and through the windows facing Market Street as Mack hailed a cab, helped Suzy get in, and closed the door for her.

A few moments later, the two men were back at their table, both sipping coffee.

"So...," said Nick. "You and Suzy?"

"Sure. Once you get her undressed, she's a lot of fun in bed." Mack grinned. "Besides, she's almost better than you at—"

"No one is better than me at that. Ask Carter. Ask Jeffery." Nick was blushing but, truth be told, he had learned a lot in the Navy. Quite a lot, in fact.

"*Ask all the men in the barracks...*" Mack was singing in a voice just above a whisper.

"What the hell is that?"

"You never heard that little ditty before?"

"No."

With a big grin, Mack softly sang:

Ask all the men in the barracks...
They'll tell you 'bout tail and it's right!
Best to shove it up into the carracks...
Of the boys in the blue and the white!

The images those words brought up in his mind made Nick start laughing and hard. He put his fist in his mouth and bit down to keep from making too much noise. Once he finally got hold of himself, he took a couple of deep breaths and then quietly asked, "*Carracks*? Where in the hell did you learn that one?"

"From some Army guys in Hawaii. Right before I took one of 'em out and showed him how the Navy goes both ways." He pointed his thick index finger at Nick and pretended to shoot him with it. "Pow!"

Nick started laughing again. Mack joined right in until an older man two tables over hushed them with a sharp word ("*Please!*") and a disapproving frown.

Hanging their heads, they both giggled as soft as they could for a minute or two before Nick got up so he could hit the head.

. . .

Mack sat back in his chair and studied his friend for a moment. When he got like that, Nick was always tempted to ask him what was running through his mind. He never did, since he tended to enjoy watching the wheels turn more than anything else.

Finally, Mack took a long sip of his coffee and then asked, "One more Camel for the road?"

Nick obliged. He was tempted to have one more himself, but he thought he'd had enough for the evening.

Mack considered his cigarette for a moment before saying, "Well, I guess I'm gonna say what I shoulda said back in August."

"What's that?" asked Nick.

"Congratulations."

Nick grinned. "Thanks, Mack. That means a lot coming from you."

Mack took a long drag and then pointed his mouth towards the ceiling and exhaled a couple of smoke rings. "Whenever you talk about Carter, your beautiful brown eyes light up."

Nick nodded. He loved the fireman, there were no two ways about it.

Looking across the table, Mack's brow furrowed a little. He put both elbows on the table and then held his Camel in front of his mouth to take another puff. After exhaling to the right, he said, "I just don't wanna see you get hurt like you did with Jeffery."

"Carter's not like that."

Nodding, Mack said, "I can see that."

Before he could stop himself, Nick asked, "Why aren't we together?"

"Come again?"

"Why didn't we ever go any further than just being friends who were having a good time?"

Mack looked over Nick's head for a long moment and then said, "Did I tell you I got me a new job starting tomorrow?"

"Where?" asked Nick, resigning himself to never getting an answer to his previous question. He'd asked before and gotten the same answer: nothing.

"For a construction company building a row of houses in the Sunset." Mack took one last draw in his cigarette and then stubbed it out in the ashtray. He abruptly stood. "Well, I gotta go."

Nick put down his cup and got up. He reached into his pocket, pulled out a five, and dropped it on the table "Where you headed?"

"Nowhere in particular. You?"

"The same," replied Nick as he led the way through the restaurant and outside.

The bright lights of Market Street lit the chilly night

sky as the two friends silently made their way towards the Ferry Building in the distance and to wherever they were going next that night.

Note

The little ditty that Mack sings about soldiers (or marines) and sailors is entirely of my own creation.

You can watch the Paramount/Famous Studios production of "Little Brown Jug", the cartoon Mack refers to, on YouTube. The lyrics Mack sings are the original ones, however, as written by Joseph Eastburn Winner in 1869.

Mardi Gras 1975

Chapter 1

835 Dumaine St.
New Orleans, LA 70116
Tuesday, February 11, 1975
Just past dawn

The thump-thump of a song was coming through the wall next to the bed as I opened my eyes. I looked at my watch. It was half past 6 in the morning. I put my left arm over my eyes to keep out the light.

I could feel the daiquiris from the night before sitting on my head like a heavy iron fist. And the thump-thump wasn't helping.

I banged on the wall. That didn't do anything other than make Carter turn over and ask, "What the hell, Nick?"

Carter Jones was my tall, muscular ex-fireman of a husband and he was sleeping next to me on the double bed in the second-floor bedroom of the little house we'd bought a few weeks earlier in the French Quarter of New Orleans.

"Damn hippies next door have their goddam record player too loud."

"Like I told you before, they're not hippies. They live on some commune in Tennessee."

I sighed and put my arm over my eyes, trying to block the blinding sunlight coming through the blinds. "They have dirty feet like hippies."

"Hippies are straight. These kids are gay. They call themselves fairies."

"I don't care if they fuck sheep, they're dirty. And they woke me up."

Carter laughed and kissed me on my belly. "You'll feel better once you get some coffee. Let's head over to the Clover Grille and get some grease."

I asked, "Do you have a hangover?"

"No, son, because I remembered to take aspirin last night. I tried to give you some, but you told me to go fuck myself."

I laughed, which hurt. "Did you?"

Carter pulled on my right arm and said, "Get up. I'm hungry."

I sat up and covered my eyes. "It's so bright in here."

"You must be hurtin', son, cause it's foggy outside."

"Ugh," was the only answer I could come up with right then.

. . .

As we staggered down Dumaine Street, I asked, "What did we do last night?"

Carter put his arm around my shoulder. "Well, we went to one of those private parties in the Garden District."

"We did?"

"Yep. And you guzzled way too many daiquiris and that's why you feel like hell."

As I kicked a brown beer bottle into the street and winced from the sound of it clanging, I asked, "What time did we go to bed?"

"A little after 11."

Right then, we walked past the open doors of Lafitte's in Exile, a gay bar at the corner of Bourbon Street where we'd had some swell times, particularly on a trip back in '62. The song playing over the loudspeakers was "Get Dancin'" by Disco-Tex and the Sex-O-Lettes. It had been one of the songs playing everywhere we'd gone in the past couple of days.

As we stood at the corner and waited for a long line of sanitation trucks to make their way past, I got a big whiff of what I had decided to call "New Orleans During Mardi Gras." It was a mix of stale cigarette smoke, stale beer, stale vomit, and disinfectant. My stomach turned so I held onto Carter's arm.

He put his hand on mine. "You OK there, Boss?"

I nodded. "Yeah. Doesn't the smell get to you?"

He laughed. "Haven't you seen me putting Vicks under my nose?" By then the trucks had rumbled past. We carefully stepped into the trash-riddled street.

"Is that what's in that little tube?"

"You got it. I can't smell anything but eucalyptus and camphor or whatever the hell they use."

As we made our way through the front door of the Clover Grille, I saw Henry and Robert sitting in the back booth. Henry Winters was Carter's first lover and a good friend to us both. Robert Evans was his lover and the man who managed my real estate among other things. They'd been together for 22 years. Carter always claimed Henry and I looked alike which was ridiculous since Henry was much more handsome than me.

As we moved towards the back of the room, I could see that was Robert was his usually cheery self. But Henry looked as bad as I felt.

We slid in across from them as the waiter walked up. He asked, "Coffee and water?"

I asked, "Any chance for an Alka-Seltzer?"

Carter jumped in and said, "Nope. Just bring us coffee and water. And we're ready to order, if that's OK."

The waiter, a dark-haired kid with a short haircut smiled at Carter. "Sure thing, Daddy. What'll it be?"

"Two eggs over easy, chewy bacon, crispy hash browns, buttered rye toast. And two of those. One for me and one for my husband, here."

As the waiter wrote down our order, he raised an eyebrow. "Husband?"

"Yeah," I replied. "And I'm in pain."

"Well," snapped the waiter. "I'll get right on that." He turned on his heel and called out our order as he walked towards the kitchen.

I looked at Henry who shook his head. "Nick, you better hope that he doesn't spit in your food."

I tried to grin, but it hurt too much. "I don't think spit is gonna hurt the food here."

Robert asked, "So, did you two go to that private party last night?"

Carter nodded. "Yep. I wish you guys had come with us instead of staying in. Believe it or not, we were the youngest guys there."

"We were?" I asked.

Pointing at me with his left thumb, Carter said, "This one doesn't remember a thing. He had about five daiquiris too many."

I groaned and slouched down in the booth. "Be nice to me, Carter Jones."

"I am being nice to you, Nicholas Williams. I ordered

your breakfast for you. And I warned off the waiter. What more do you want?"

"A kiss on the cheek."

Carter turned and did just that.

...

Once I'd eaten and had a full glass of water, along with two cups of coffee, I was beginning to feel like I might live.

Henry, who was smoking a Kent, looked at me. "Did we tell you about seeing Robert's nephew and his kids?"

I shook my head over my third cup of coffee. "When was that?"

Robert said, "Two weeks ago. We drove up to Ukiah and spent a couple of days with them."

Henry leaned forward conspiratorially. "They live in a yurt."

"What's a yurt?" I asked.

"It's a big round tent like shepherds use in Mongolia. And it smelled like sheep lived there. I kept looking around for one but never found any."

Carter and I laughed as Robert rolled his eyes. He said, "Some people don't like buildings without corners."

Henry tapped his cigarette on the edge of the ashtray. "Or floors. Ukiah isn't Mongolia. And those kids run wild. Billy, that's the nephew, and Sunflower, that's his wife." He took a drag on his cigarette. "Excuse me, his *partner*. They both took pains to explain to me how they were equals, just like Robert and me." He shook his head and continued, "None of them wore any shoes the whole time we were there. In January! In the redwoods! It was cold up there!"

Carter laughed and asked Robert, "Cal must be about 9 by now, right?"

Robert nodded. "Yes, and as smart a kid as I've ever met. Reminds me a lot of Walter." That was Walter Marcello. He ran the intelligence division of our company.

"Only taller," added Henry. Walter only stood about five feet even.

"What about Susan?" asked Carter.

Henry said, "I think you mean Moonflower, right?"

Robert rolled his eyes again. "She's fine. She's 12 and pretty headstrong. I like her."

"Who gave her that name?" I asked.

Henry snapped, "She did. I tell you, Nick, it's amazing those kids can even feed and dress themselves." He took a last drag off his Kent and then stubbed it out in the ashtray.

I glanced over at Carter who said, "Now Nick is gonna bitch about the kids who are holed up in the house next to ours."

I sighed. "No, I'm not."

"Hippies?" asked Henry.

Robert said, "There are no hippies anymore. I told you that."

"Then what do you call kids who run around the public streets without any shoes on?"

Robert shrugged. "I call them free spirits. And I admire them."

Henry pulled out another Kent. I grabbed my old beat-up Zippo from my pocket and offered it to him. He lit his cigarette and looked at the lighter. "Hell, Nick, I can't believe this old relic still works." He snapped it closed and handed it to me. "It must be older than either Billy or Sunflower."

I dropped it back in my pocket and smiled. "It's from 1941, so probably."

Robert nodded. "Billy was born in '45. He was 18 when Sunflower got pregnant with Moonflower."

"Listen to yourself, hon," said Henry. "You sound like one of them."

Robert turned on his lover and said, "Just because you were born a middle-aged man doesn't mean any of the rest of us are as old and cranky as you."

I put my elbows on the table. "Well, you're the youngest of us here, Robert. Weren't you born in '27?"

He nodded. "I'll be 48 in April." He shook his head. "Oh my God, how did this happen? It seems like it was just yesterday when I met you, Nick."

I laughed. "I know. When did you start working for Jeffery?" I was referring to Jeffery Klein, Esquire, my second lover who'd been murdered in '67. He'd been a lawyer, which is how I first met him. Robert had worked as his receptionist before he started working for me.

"1951. Right after I graduated from Cal."

Carter added, "And y'all got together on Halloween of 1953. Remember?"

Henry relaxed a little and said, "Yes. I'll never forget that night. We were all sitting in your dining room on Hartford and Robert looked at me."

"Was it love at first sight?" I asked.

He shook his head. "Not at first sight. But it didn't take long." He leaned over and kissed Robert on the cheek. "Best thing that ever happened to me."

"OK, girls, break it up. Lilly Law is here." We all looked up to see Miss Wanna Man, one of the local drag queens, standing at the table. She was about 6'2" in heels and had dark black skin with shining black eyes. By day, she worked for the City of New Orleans as a file clerk under the name Martin Jenkins but, by night, she roamed the Quarter as Miss Wanna Man. Or that's what she'd told us on Sunday night when we'd met her across the street at Lafitte's.

Carter stood and said, "Let me get you a chair, Miss Wanna."

She shook her head. "No, thank you, Mr. Jones." She kissed him on the cheek and said, "I have to fly like the ever-present wind." She sighed. "Except down here in the Quarter, the wind never blows." She then giggled and pulled on her dress. It was a dark blue number that was cut like it was from the late 60s and stopped about mid-thigh. She was wearing bright green Mardi Gras beads around her neck like a pearl choker. "But there's lots of blowin' goin' on down here, that's for damn sure."

Carter sat as we all laughed.

Robert asked, "You want anything to eat or drink, Miss Wanna?"

"No, child. I'm flyin' high on some leftover party pills and I'm afraid if I have even a sip of water, my whole house of cards will collapse, and I'll miss the party." She looked at me. "I heard Miss Nick, here, did go and get herself mightily drunk last night on daiquiris. That right, child?"

I grinned and nodded. "Yeah. And I can feel it today. How'd you know?"

She waved her hand at me. She was wearing press-on nails that had been painted electric blue. "Oh, honey, what I don't know about the Quarter ain't worth knowin'." She leaned forward and, in a stage whisper, she added, "But you better stay away from the geriatric set in the Garden District, honey. They go for blood. They'll snatch your wig twice and you won't even know you've done been made bald, if you get my drift."

I laughed. "Why do you say that?"

Lowering her voice a little more. "The rumor is that you're some sort of millionaire, billionaire, zillionaire."

She waved her hand again. "I don't even know, honey. But they say you shit money and wipe your ass with stocks and bonds and, well, some people just aren't nice, now are they?"

The four of us burst out laughing at that. Carter said, "Well, Nick is kinda rich."

Miss Wanna stood up straight. "Honey, rich or poor, don't make no matter to me. I steer clear of those whiter-than-white types uptown. They give me gas. And they don't like no nigger like me runnin' my mouth and readin' their beads. So, they stay up there and I stay down here and we're all just as happy as clams." She winked at me. "But watch your back, honey chile. You pissed Miss Regina off, but good, and, like I said, she is after blood."

Carter asked, "Who is Miss Regina?"

Miss Wanna put her hand to her chest and said, "Good God, who are these heathens? Save me!" She leaned forward and looked towards the door of the cafe before turning to Carter. "Mr. Reginald Beauregard Jackson, the Third, if you please. His great-granddaddy was a General, or somethin' like that, in the Civil War and, I have no doubt, that some of my people once worked for his people and didn't none of them get paid, if you take my meanin'."

Carter nodded. "That's whose house we went to last night." He grinned. "Reggie Jackson."

Miss Wanna shook her finger vigorously. "Uh, uh. No, ma'am. No, sir. Don't you call Miss Regina by that illustrious name." Dropping down to an actual whisper, she added, "I will gladly take a Greyhound bus to Oakland to the ballpark and take Mr. Reggie Jackson in my mouth and bring him to heaven." She sighed. "All he has to do is ask."

I laughed. "I'll tell him the next time I see him."

Miss Wanna grabbed her chest with her left hand and lifted her right hand up in the air. "Oh, Lord! Oh, sweet Jesus! Here that, Elizabeth? I'm comin' to join you honey!" We all laughed as she staggered. After a couple of beats, her demeanor changed, and she looked down at me. "You better not be lyin' to me, Miss Nick, honey. Or I'm gonna stick my size 12 heel right up your ass. Do you really know Mr. Reggie Jackson?"

I nodded with a grin. "I've met him. Carter and I both have."

Carter said, "He's a nice guy but he's a straight arrow."

Miss Wanna took Carter's right hand in her left and patted it with her right. "Oh, darlin', there hasn't been the man yet that I haven't sent to heaven. Don't talk to me about straight or bi or gay. All men like it when you make 'em feel good." She looked down at Robert. "Ain't that right, honey?"

Robert blushed and shrugged. "I don't really know."

Miss Wanna put her hand under Robert's chin and lifted it up a couple of inches. "Give me fifteen minutes, and I will take you to heaven, honey." She looked at Henry, who was scowling. Dropping her hand, she stepped back and said, "Don't you practice your voodoo on me, girl. I know real witches that can put a pin in a doll, and you'll drop dead on Ursulines Avenue, just like my dear friend, Miss Bella Ball. The *Times-Picayune* said it was a heart attack, but I knew better. It was Mistress Josephine in the Lower Ninth Ward. Everyone in town knows not to cross Mistress Josephine. But Miss Bella Ball did and look what happened to her." Miss Wanna crossed herself and said, "Does anyone have a watch?"

I looked at mine. "It's 7:45."

"Sweet Jesus, I have to fly!"

Carter stood and said, "May I walk you to the door?"

Miss Wanna grinned slyly at him and then looked around at me. "Won't Miss Nick get a little jealous?"

Carter shook his head. "It'll be our secret."

Miss Wanna looked at me and winked. Her expression suddenly turned serious. "Now don't you forget about Miss Regina. She's out for your blood. Be careful, honey chile. And give Mr. Reggie Jackson a big kiss for me when you see him next."

I smiled. "I will. Have a good day, Miss Wanna."

She bowed and then blew kisses at the table. "*Au revoir, mes petites.*" With that, I watched as she and Carter walked to the door and then out onto the street.

Turning back towards Henry and Robert, I saw that Henry was lighting up another Kent. He took a long drag and then exhaled. "Oh, God, I hate that kind of talk."

"What?" I asked, looking at Robert who was biting the inside of his mouth nervously.

"That 'Miss Nick' and 'her this' and 'she that'." He viciously tapped his cigarette on the ashtray. "Makes me sick to my stomach."

Robert sighed. "I like it. It's liberating."

"*Gay liberation*," sneered Henry. "Who needs it?"

I slammed the table. "We do, Henry Winters, or have you forgotten how it was?"

He gaped at me as Carter slid in next to me. He put his arm over my shoulder and asked, "What happened?"

Henry stubbed out his cigarette and said, "Nick was just about to give me a history lesson."

"In what?" asked Carter, his voice sounding dangerous.

"In gay liberation," said Robert. He turned and looked at his lover. "Bechtel fired you for being gay in

1953. Remember? Nick is the reason you're the most successful engineer on the west coast. Apologize to him, Henry."

I held up my hand. "No, Robert, that's not the point."

"What is the point?" asked Henry.

"The point is that a fabulous black man just came in here dressed in a miniskirt and was exactly who he wanted to be," said Carter. "And you, of all people, should know what that means. Not just because he's a man in a dress. But because he's a *black* man in a dress. And there're no cops around to harass him or drag him off to jail." Looking at Robert, he said, "This isn't about Nick. This is about people like your nephew and the kids in the house next door. And all those black kids who had lunch counter sit-ins and protested the war and stood up for what belonged to them. Just like those kids did in New York for us." He shook his head. "Henry, you should know better. You know what it was like in Albany and how it got worse after we left. But now it's all changed. And here we are, and I've got my arm around Nick, and I can kiss him on the street if I want. Some people might make a scene but not everyone. It is liberating. We've got our freedom. Finally."

Henry nodded. "You're right, Carter." He looked down at the table for a couple of beats. "It was awful for us and for them in Albany. And I'm sure it was like that here."

Robert added, "You know that bar that caught fire where everyone was burned alive is just a few blocks from here, right? That was just a couple of years ago. They couldn't get away with that kind of thing now. Gay liberation is here to stay."

After a long moment, Henry looked at me. "I'm sorry, Nick."

I smiled at him as Robert put his arm around Henry's shoulder and looked at me. "Truth is, we shouldn't have come. Henry doesn't like crowds. I think it's all been too much for him."

I said, "Why don't you fly home? You don't have to stay."

Henry wiped away a tear and nodded. "Maybe I will." He looked at Robert. "You stay here. Maybe I'll go to Tahoe and go skiing."

Robert pulled him close. "No, I'll go with you. I wanted to go skiing anyway."

I said, "Why don't you take the jet? We can leave on Thursday."

"You sure?" asked Henry as he buried his head into Robert's shoulder.

Carter said, "Yes. I'm glad y'all came with us. But I'd rather—"

"What is this? *Gays of Our Lives*?" That was our waiter. He slapped the check on the table. "I need y'all queens to pay and to be on your way. We've gotta line out the door."

I looked out the window and realized the street was filling up with people already. It was still foggy and gray, but the crowd was bright and festive.

Carter stood and put a hundred in the man's hand. "That should take care of it and there's no need to be nasty about it."

The waiter sighed. "Sorry, Daddy. This is the biggest day of the year."

I slid out and stood. "Sorry we took so long. We'll be going." I put another hundred in his hand and then walked towards the door.

Chapter 2

835 Dumaine St.
New Orleans, LA 70116
Tuesday, February 11, 1975
11:30 a.m.

"Do we have to?" That was me whining in response to Carter's suggestion that we accept our neighbors' invitation to lunch at their place.

We had just finished a romp in the hay, followed by a shower. Carter was pulling on his white jeans, buttoning up, and tucking in as I was watching from the edge of the bed. At some point in the last couple of days, he had found a rodeo prize belt buckle in some store in the Quarter. It was the kind that you had to attach to both ends of the belt. After fumbling with it for a moment, he looked at me. "Yes, we do. And can you help me out here?"

I stood and walked over to where he was standing. I yanked on the denim-colored belt and attached the buckle to both ends. "What shirt are you wearing?"

He grinned down at me. "If it was warmer, I wouldn't wear one at all."

I laughed. "Well, this ain't the Castro in the summer, fireman. How about the red one with the paisley pattern on it?"

He nodded. "Sure."

I walked over to the closet, pulled it off the hanger, and handed it to him.

He pulled it on and just tied it at the bottom, leaving his hairy and muscled chest exposed.

I ran my hand through the hair, noticing how many more of them were white than the last time I'd looked closely. "Now all you need are some gold chains."

"Not bad for a 55 year-old man, doncha think?"

I leaned in and put my arms around him. "How did we ever get this old?"

He pulled me in close. "I have no fucking idea but I kinda like it, don't you?"

I nodded on the hard pillow of his chest. He smelled like Irish Spring. "Yeah, I do. It's amazing we both made it this far."

He laughed and pulled back. "Now, what about shoes?"

I shook my head. "Who are you trying to impress? We're gonna eat lunch with kids who don't wear shoes, remember?"

He sighed. "But I thought you'd like for me to set a good example."

I laughed. "Don't put this on me, fireman. I know what's what. You have the hots for the chubby one." I looked up in time to catch him blushing. "He could be your son, Carter."

He shrugged. "You know how I feel about a round belly that's all hairy."

I leaned back and stuck mine out. I was only wearing my BVDs. "How's that?"

Carter sighed and rubbed it. "You still weigh within five pounds of how much you weighed when we first met. I've tried to get you to gain weight, but it never happens. You just eat and eat, and it never sticks."

"Well, Chief, I'm sorry to disappoint you..."

He kissed me on the forehead. "You know what I really mean." He ran his hand through my hair. "Besides, I saw you checking out that kid who was wearing engineer boots yesterday when we were at Lafitte's."

It was my turn to blush. "Did you see the legs on him? Almost as long as yours. And his jeans on that ass."

Carter reached around and swatted me on my ass. "I sure did. These eyes don't miss a thing."

. . .

"Come on in, you two." That was Harvey. He stood just inside the door and motioned us in. He was the taller of the couple. As we walked by, I noticed he was wearing an open white shirt with blue drawstring pants. He sported a long blond beard with equally long blond hair. A necklace of wooden beads with bits of bright yellow fabric wrapped in and around the beads were hanging down on his chest. I also noticed he wasn't wearing any shoes. His big hairy feet weren't unattractive, but I hoped I wouldn't have to see the bottoms of them while we were eating.

Harvey pulled Carter into a long hug. He made a kind of humming sound as they stood there. He released Carter and then said, "Hi, Nick." He pulled me in, wrapping his long, lean body around mine. He smelled like sandalwood, which I liked. He hummed on me for a moment and then let me go.

"Come on back. Devon is cooking some red beans and brown rice. Vegetarian, of course. Hope you like garlic."

Carter, who tolerated garlic but didn't much care for it, was polite and said, "Smells good."

We walked into their living room. It was mostly just big piles of pillows scattered everywhere. There was a big round table in the middle of the floor. Its top was about two feet off the ground, and it was set with four places.

Harvey looked down at my shoes, which were Bass Weejuns, the kind with the penny, and said, "Kick off your shoes, if you don't mind, and leave them in the hallway. And have a seat wherever is comfortable. Would you like some limeade? We make it with honey. White sugar is a real killer."

I nodded as I took off my shoes. I leaned over to pick them up and then grabbed Carter's canvas sneakers. I carried them both into the entryway and said, "That sounds good, Harvey."

Carter said, "I'll just have some water, if that's OK."

As I walked back into the living room, Harvey said, "Oh, sure, man. That's fine. Y'all have a seat and I'll be right back."

He patted me on the head as he walked past me and made a ding sound as he did. Once he was in the kitchen, I asked Carter in a whisper, "What the fuck?"

He grinned and whispered back. "He's just a kid. Can't be even 30 yet."

"Hard to tell under all that hair."

"Now you sound like Henry."

I snorted. "I forgot to ask. What did he say when he called?"

"That they were getting on the jet at 11 and that it should be back here tomorrow by noon so we can leave whenever." He looked down at me. "You're doing that thing."

"What thing?"

"Where you get uptight. Remember what we talked about?"

I sighed and rolled my eyes. "Fine. I'll think about you rubbing my belly."

He grinned. "Now I'm thinking about it." He put his hand up my shirt and began to rub. "Doesn't that feel better?"

I sighed and then nodded. "Yeah, it does."

"One of these days, I'm gonna give you a lid and—"

Before he could finish telling me, one more time, how he was gonna blow my mind, Harvey walked into the living room with a tray of drinks. Three were light green with ice and one was plain water.

"Y'all have a seat. Devon is filling the bowls and will be out in a minute." As he set out the glasses on the table, Carter and I both sat on the floor and crossed our legs. I pulled mine up close. As Carter wiggled around on some pillows, I heard his jeans rip.

I fell back on the pile of pillows behind me and started laughing so hard that I began to snort.

Harvey said, "Oh, Carter! Are you OK?"

Carter rolled over and got on top of me, pinning my arms to the floor. "I'm fine, Harvey. It's Nick who's in a lot of trouble."

. . .

It only took me a couple of minutes to run next door and get him a fresh pair of blue jeans. I managed to snort and giggle the entire time as the sound of the rip played again and again in my head.

Once I was back, I found Carter standing in the middle of the living room in his underwear and red shirt. He was talking to Harvey while Devon was standing by the kitchen door, frozen as he took in the sight of Carter's thick muscled legs, all covered in blond hair, and the big package that sat at the top of them. The table was already set with four big steaming bowls.

"I don't know that much about Ford," said Carter. "I try to stay out of things like that these days."

I walked in and said, "Here're your blue jeans, Carter." He grinned at me and took them from my outstretched hand. Once he had them on, I asked, "What about your belt?"

He waved me away. "That can wait. I'm hungry." He looked over at Devon, who was still frozen by the kitchen door. "This sure smells good."

The chubby kid smiled. He was about 5'7" with brown hair and brown eyes and was wearing a long shirt with an interesting pattern on it. It was a dark brown. The pattern was white and reminded me of Africa, for some reason. His sleeves were rolled up, revealing hairy arms. Under his shirt, he was wearing cotton pants that were the same color as Harvey's. As Carter spoke, he moved a little closer, as shy as a deer.

I walked over and put my arm around his shoulder. He smelled like garlic and sandalwood. He was wearing the same kind of beads that Harvey had on. "Come on, Devon. Let's go eat."

He nodded but didn't say anything. He let me lead him into the living room. Once we were there, I sat down between Harvey and Carter, leaving the space opposite me open for him to take. Much to my surprise, he sat down gracefully and crossed his legs.

Devon and Harvey held out their hands as if they wanted us to take them and make a circle. Carter and I followed their lead. Devon and Harvey then closed their eyes.

Harvey said, "Mother, Father, Creator, thank you for this bountiful meal from your abundant nature. And thank you for new friends and the joy of their company." He paused. He then squeezed my hand and said, "And so it is."

Devon repeated that and then they both opened their eyes and let go. Devon sighed and said, "Dig in, y'all." They both had southern twangs, but Devon's was definitely more pronounced.

Carter and I picked up our spoons. I scooped up a bite and then blew on my spoon to let the rice and beans cool a little. I took a bite and was surprised. It tasted good. The garlic was there but it wasn't strong. There was something else, some other flavor, but I couldn't figure out what it was, so I had another bite. Looking over at Devon, I asked, "What's that other flavor? I can taste onion and garlic but there's something else. What is it?"

"Oh, it's probably the amino acids," he replied. "I always add some Bragg's to most everything."

Carter nodded. "That's what I thought it was." He looked at me. "Jack LaLanne swears by this stuff."

I tried not to roll my eyes. Jack was a fitness expert who had a fitness-oriented TV show that broadcast out of San Francisco. He was about five years older than Carter and, as far as I was concerned, was a little too much of a self promoter. Carter liked him, although he didn't always agree with Jack's diet ideas.

Devon vigorously nodded his head. "Did you know Jack got his start after attending one of Dr. Bragg's lectures?"

Carter smiled. "That's what he told me."

Devon's eyes widened. "You know him?"

"Sure do. I met him not long after I moved to San Francisco back in 1939."

"Wow, Carter. Is he as handsome in real life as he is on TV?"

I tried not to laugh as Carter smiled. "He's a little fireplug of a guy, which doesn't always show on TV. He's shorter than you. And, I guess you could say he's handsome, but he's married. His wife, Elaine, is a nice gal."

Devon sighed as Harvey frowned into his bowl while slowly stirring the beans and rice together.

"Where are you two from, originally?" I asked.

Devon said, "I grew up in Jackson, Mississippi." He pursed his lips. "I hated it there."

"And you, Harvey?"

"I'm from Atlanta," he replied.

Carter grinned. "I thought you were a Georgia boy, just like me."

Harvey smiled a little. "Where are you from, Carter?"

"Albany."

Harvey laughed. "Don't you mean *Albinny*?"

Nodding, Carter smiled. "You must have met someone from there."

"My mom grew up there."

Carter tilted his head. "What's her name?"

"Mary-Lynn Bosworth."

Carter frowned. "What was her maiden name?"

"Johnson."

I coughed. "Oh, dear God! You're not related to the Johnson family in Albany, are you?"

Harvey looked over at me with a big frown. "I guess. I don't really know any of my relations in the area."

Carter shook his head. "Count yourself lucky, son. Your grandfather and my daddy almost killed each other once upon a time."

"Really?"

I glanced over at Devon who was looking alarmed. I said, "Don't worry, Devon. This is ancient history."

He nodded but didn't look relieved.

Carter continued, "Yeah. There's some bad blood from back then. I'm surprised your mama never told you about your Aunt Eileen."

Harvey's frown deepened. "I don't have an Aunt Eileen."

"Your grandfather was William Johnson, right? Big Bill?"

Harvey nodded. "I never met him. But his name was William."

"And your mother has about the same color hair as you?"

He nodded. "Not anymore, but she did when I was little."

"There was only one white William Johnson in Albany. There were two who were black. But only one was white. And he was a pretty mean dude."

Harvey nodded again. "That sounds right. My mother hated that town. She always said she couldn't wait to get away."

Carter said, "I felt the same way."

"Did you ever go back?" asked Devon.

"A few times. But the most famous time was when my daddy was killed at the lumber mill."

Harvey sat back. "That was your father?"

Carter nodded. "You've heard about that story?"

Harvey sighed. "Yeah. My mother told me there was a really horrible man who was murdered at the sawmill and that she hated him and would have done it herself."

Carter leaned forward. "Did she say why?"

Harvey shook his head. "She won't say. I've asked her a couple of times to tell me more, but she won't talk about it."

"That's probably just as well."

"What was your father's name?" asked Devon.

"Wilson Jones," replied Carter with some heat in his voice.

I reached over and put my hand on his arm. He nodded and put down his spoon. I could feel him relax. He was really good at being able to make himself relax on command. It had something to do with meditation. I didn't understand it all, or even really believe in it, but it worked for him and that was all that mattered.

I said, "It's a long story but we both went to Albany to figure out who killed Carter's father. That was in the summer of '53. And that's when I first met Carter's mother."

Devon looked over at Harvey. "I met Mary-Lynn last summer. We hitchhiked down to Atlanta from Tennessee and we stayed with her for a couple of weeks."

Carter looked at Harvey. "Do you have any brothers or sisters?"

He shook his head. "Just me. And my old man packed up and shipped out a long time ago. So it was just me and mama for a while. Then I graduated high school and decided to go to Tennessee, the university, that is, for school. I dropped out in '69 and came out in '70. I bought a little bit of land using some dough my old man had left for me and that's where Devon and I live when we're there."

"What about this place?" I asked.

"This is mine," said Devon. He looked at Harvey. "Well, it's ours. But it's in my name. I bought it in '68 and was living here full time until I met Harvey in '71."

"How'd y'all meet?" asked Carter.

Devon looked down at his bowl and stirred his spoon slowly, just like Harvey had done earlier. After a moment, Harvey said, "We met at a bus station in Atlanta."

Carter grinned. "Were you there for the bus or...?"

Harvey sighed. "The other. I was visiting my mama

and needed some relief, so I went down to the Greyhound station downtown because..." He shrugged. "That's where everyone used to go."

Devon said, "I was there waiting for a bus to Knoxville."

Harvey smiled. "If I'd have waited a week or two, we probably would have met there. That's where our property is."

"It's about thirty miles out of town," added Devon. "Out in the country."

"Why were you headed to Knoxville?" asked Carter.

Devon sighed and stirred his bowl again.

Harvey said, "He doesn't like to talk about it, but I think you two would be down for a story like this."

Carter and I both nodded. I wondered what was so mysterious.

Harvey drank some of his limeade and then said, "Devon had a vision."

Devon sighed and whispered, "*Harvey*."

Carter piped up. "I get it. I've had visions."

Looking up, Devon asked, "You have?"

"Sure. It's been a while. But I get it. What was your vision?"

Devon shrugged. "Just to buy a bus ticket from here to Knoxville. I had no idea why, but it seemed really important."

"Was it drug-induced?" asked Carter.

Looking offended, Devon shook his head. "No, never. I was meditating and I saw a bus ticket and it said Knoxville. And every time I sat down to meditate, I would see it."

"How long did that go on?"

"About a week. Then it started waking me up. So, finally, I told the Universe to stop hassling me and I went down and got a ticket and got on the bus..." He looked at Harvey and smiled. "And here we are."

I nodded and grinned. "Here you are."

Carter put his arm on my leg. "Devon, you have no idea how happy you just made Nick. He loves stories like this."

I nodded. "I do. I really do."

. . .

After lunch, I helped Devon clean up and do the dishes. We then moved over to our apartment. We had a balcony and could see a little sliver of Bourbon Street. The party was already happening, and it had spilled onto our street. So the four of us sat up there and watched the world go by on Dumaine Street below.

"How often do you two come to New Orleans?" I asked.

"We usually spend the winter here," said Harvey. He was sipping some kind of green tea from a mug. "We have a stove in Tennessee but that's it for heat. Besides, we both like Mardi Gras."

Carter said, "I thought you lived in a commune and called yourself fairies or something like that."

Devon looked out over the crowd. "Something like that. We don't like to talk about it. It's nobody's business." He didn't sound defensive. I wondered about that.

Carter nodded thoughtfully. "When do you go back to Tennessee?"

"Whenever we get the urge," replied Harvey.

Carter grinned. "I like that."

I asked Devon, "What about your family?"

He shook his head. "I don't talk to them since they don't talk to me."

"Sorry to hear that."

He shrugged. "It's no sweat. I never fit in with them and I think they were glad to get rid of me." He looked over at Harvey. "Besides, I have Harvey and Mary-Lynn said I could call her my mother. And she is."

"What about your father?" asked Carter in a curiously subdued voice.

Devon looked over at Carter. "We father each other."

I nodded. "That's what I did with my first lover."

"Really?" asked Devon.

"Yeah. His name is Mike and he took me in when my old man kicked me out of the house in '39. I lived with him until the war started and then I signed up."

Harvey squirmed in his chair. "I like you, Nick, so I hope you don't me asking why you went to war?"

I nodded. "It was a different war. We lived in San Francisco. It seemed like the Japanese were just over the horizon, ready to bomb us like they did Hawaii. It was different."

Harvey looked at his tea. "But I heard that FDR provoked the Japanese into bombing Pearl Harbor."

"I don't know about that. And it was all a long time ago."

Carter piped up. "I wish I'd gone."

Devon asked, "Really?"

Carter nodded. "Sure. I was asked not to sign up. I was a fireman and they wanted us to stay home in case the Japanese bombed the City."

Devon nodded. "Makes sense."

Harvey sighed but didn't say anything.

Devon asked, "What do you do now, Carter?"

I grinned a little. There had been a time when we couldn't go anywhere without being recognized. We were in the papers so often that people would know who we were even when we tried to disguise ourselves. But in the last ten or so years, that had changed. Outside of San Francisco, at least. And I was happy that it had. It was good to be able to go somewhere and for no one to know who we were or, if they did recognize us, not to care much about it, one way or another.

Carter replied, "Nick and I own a company."

"You do?" asked Devon. "Have we heard of it?"

"What about Monumental Studios? Ever heard of that?" I asked.

Both Devon and Harvey nodded. They also both exchanged a glance.

Carter said, "We own it."

Devon squealed a little. He put his hand on his chest and asked, "Do you know Tommy Davis?" He was a very popular leading man.

I grinned. "Yeah. Did you see *Burning Man Running*?" It was the latest Monumental movie. It had come out at the beginning of the year.

Devon nodded and looked at Harvey. "We loved it!"

I said, "Carter has a cameo in it."

"You do?" asked Devon, his mouth hanging open.

Carter nodded. "I'm the priest."

Harvey sat up. "You're shitting me, man!"

Carter laughed and shook his head. "No, I'm not."

Devon had his hand over his mouth and was looking from Carter to me and then back to Carter. "Oh my God. I can't believe I'm sitting here with Father Ryan." His eyes were bulging out and he was bouncing up and down in his chair.

Harvey, whose face was red, said, "Man, you have no idea how many times I've beat off to you."

Devon nodded. "Yeah, me too. That scene with you in that place. Oh, man, that scene."

I laughed and said, "Me too."

Blushing hard, Carter said, "I had no idea."

"Have you seen it?" asked Harvey.

Carter shook his head. "Nick went and saw it without me. I was too embarrassed."

I leaned forward. "Remember what I told you about the camera angles?"

He nodded.

"Remember how Ben used to do that thing with Pete? And Bill Powers?"

Carter leaned over and put his face in his hands. "Nick, why didn't you tell me?"

I put my hand on his back. "Sorry, Chief. I tried to but—"

Devon, who was bouncing up and down, blurted out. "You know Bill Powers, too?"

I looked over Carter's back at him and grinned. "Sure."

Harvey shook his head. "Mama is gonna split a gut when she hears about this. She was in love with Bill Powers. This is cosmic."

Devon sighed and nodded, as the crowd below passed by. "Yeah, man. Cosmic."

Chapter 3

835 Dumaine St.
New Orleans, LA 70116
Tuesday, February 11, 1975
7:15 p.m.

"I hope you like canned soup." That was me yelling to Carter from the kitchen. We hadn't planned things very well. We'd both been thinking we could go out somewhere nice for dinner. We hadn't thought about how hard it would be to move two or three blocks in any direction. So, after trying to find someplace to eat, we'd ended up back at the house with me going through the kitchen trying to figure out what we could eat.

"That's fine," said Carter as he walked through the door from the dining room. "We have any crackers?"

"Yeah. Saltines and four cans of cream of tomato. That OK?"

"Sure. Let's eat and then head down to Lafitte's. We can watch the crowd from there." He walked up behind me and grabbed me by the waist. Pulling me in against his crotch, he whispered, "Then, when we've had enough, we can come home, and you and Father Ryan can go at it."

I turned around and looked up at him. The white hairs in his otherwise blond hair seemed to be multiplying. Or maybe it was a trick of the light. I grinned. "I think it's Father Ryan who'll be going at it, Chief."

Carter leaned down and gently bit my ear. He growled and then kissed me deeply, plunging his tongue into my mouth.

. . .

As we were washing up after dinner, I said, "Can you believe that Harvey is a Johnson from Albany?"

Carter was drying a bowl. He snorted. "I'm surprised we don't run into one of them everywhere we go. They're like rabbits. They pop up everywhere."

I nodded. "I wonder what John and Roger will say when you tell them?" John Parker was Carter's cousin and Roger Johnson, of the same clan, was John's lover. They both lived in Seattle where John ran the regional division of our security business. Roger was teaching English at one of the high schools there.

"Well, that ought to be interesting because I think John went with Mary-Lynn in high school."

"Then she and Eileen must have been close in age," I said as I rinsed out the sink.

"Mary-Lynn was a year ahead of me and a year behind John."

"I always forget that he's older than you."

"He's Mike's age, or close to it."

"No, I don't think so. Mike was born in '15. John was born in '18, right?"

"Yep. His daddy passed from the influenza right before he was born."

I nodded. "I thought that's what your mother had said."

Carter nodded and didn't say anything.

"How you doin'?"

He smiled at me. "OK. It's still amazing to me how much I miss her. We never really did..."

I put down my towel and took his right hand. Squeezing it, I said, "Yes, you did. I know you think you didn't, but you did. You did. She did as much as she could, but you were the one who did all the work. Don't forget that, Carter." Louise, his mother, had passed away back in '65.

He sniffed. I took the towel out of his hand and wiped the tears from his face. "You know," he said as he kissed me on the forehead, "I think about Ed more than I do Mama." Ed was Carter's stepfather and had been married to Louise when she died. He'd passed away in '70. He'd also been in a relationship with my mother back in the 40s. When we'd discovered what had really happened to my mother in the winter of '55, that was when Ed and Louise had met and gotten married. It had been a wonderful thing.

I nodded. "I think about Ed a lot, too. I miss him."

Carter sighed and looked down at me. "I'm getting old, Nick. People keep dying."

I nodded. "I know what you mean."

. . .

As we moved through the crowd along Dumaine and headed towards Lafitte's, I said to Carter, "You'd think this weather would have made some people stay inside." It was a little chilly and drizzling.

A woman walking near us heard me and, in a thick accent, replied, "Oh, honey, it's Mardi Gras! Fat Tuesday! It could be snowin' and everyone would still be here!" She let out a holler, which made everyone around us start to whoop and holler as well.

Carter put his hand on my shoulder. "You heard the lady. It's Mardi Gras, son!"

. . .

Lafitte's was packed, of course. We somehow made it to the bar and found Rick, the bartender who'd taken care of us every night since we'd arrived. He grinned up at Carter. "Isn't this crazy? I love it!"

I realized that "Get Dancin'" by Disco-Tex was playing again and pointed up. "This song!" I said as Rick poured some dark rum into three shot glasses.

He grinned. "I love it! I could listen to it all night."

I mumbled, "You probably will."

He picked up a shot glass and said, "Happy Mardi Gras, guys!" as he drank it.

We followed his lead and quickly knocked back the rum. Carter put his glass down on the bar and then leaned forward, a folded hundred in his outstretched hand. "From now on, just beer. Preferably watery beer. Neither of us is gonna last very long."

Rick quickly stuffed the hundred in his jeans and grinned. "Anything you say, man. You're the boss."

He reached down and pulled two bottles of Jax beer from the cooler, popped the lids, and said, "Here you go."

I took mine and then followed as Carter grabbed his and began to move through the crowd. I had learned over the years to just let him push through crowds, wherever we were. Besides being stronger, he was six inches taller and twice as wide as I was. All I had to do was follow and let him do all the work.

Carter led me to a spot right by a pillar near the corner of the building. We were a few feet above the street and had a great view. He pulled me around so that I was standing in front of him, facing the street, and then held me tight across the chest with one hand as he drank his beer with the other. All I had to do was lean back and—

Smack! Out of nowhere, someone slapped me across the face. I was so shocked, that I dropped my bottle and heard it crack on the pavement. There was a blond man in front of me who turned and looked at me accusingly. "Hey!" he said.

"Sorry," I replied as I rubbed my face.

He frowned and leaned forward, looking at my cheek. "You OK? Someone hit you?"

I nodded. "Yeah. That's why I dropped my beer. You see anyone?"

He shook his head and then looked above me at Carter. "Was it that guy?"

"What guy?" asked Carter.

"You," said the man, his eyes narrowing.

"Me, who?"

I tugged on Carter's protective arm, so he we would let me go long enough to turn around. In all the noise, I doubted he would be able to hear me. He let go a little and I turned around. He looked down at me and frowned. "What happened?"

"Someone hit me."

Holding his beer bottle off to the side, he ran his thumb along my cheek. "With a bottle or a can?"

I shook my head. "No, they slapped me." I felt someone tap me on my shoulder.

It was the guy I'd dropped the bottle on. He asked, "You OK?"

I nodded and turned around in the tight space. Looking down at him, I said, "Yeah. He's my husband."

He grinned. "Husband? You mean your lover?"

I nodded. "Sure. We've always called each other husband, though." When I said that, I felt Carter pull me in tightly. He leaned down and kissed me on the neck.

"I *am* your husband," he whispered.

I nodded as he pushed his crotch against my lower back and gave me another reminder of why that was true. I laughed.

The guy in front of me asked, "What's so funny?"

I shook my head. "Nothing. You sure you didn't see anyone?"

"No, I didn't. Sorry." He looked at me longingly for a moment. He was about 35, from what I could see in the light. And he wasn't unattractive. Just too young for me, by far. The biggest strike against him was that he wasn't Carter.

After a moment, he sighed and said, "See ya later."

I smiled. "Sure. Go out there and try and get into some trouble. This is the night for it."

He looked around. "Seems like everyone's here in a group. I'm by myself."

Carter leaned forward over my shoulder. "You can hang out with us, if you want."

"Really?" asked the man.

Carter nodded. "I'm Carter and this is Nick." He tapped on my chest.

The man smiled. He had a sweet smile. "I'm Jerry. I'm from San Diego. Where do you guys live?"

"San Francisco," replied Carter.

He nodded. "Frisco. Love that place."

Carter said, "Careful, Jerry."

"What?" asked the man as he took a drink from his plastic cup.

I said, "We never call it Frisco. Always San Francisco. It's a thing."

He shrugged. "Sure. I get it. So why are you two here?"

Carter said, "We thought it would be fun."

"Lots of guys here," said Jerry.

I nodded. "Yeah. But, for me, there's only one guy."

Jerry immediately looked disappointed.

Carter leaned down. "This is your lucky day, Jerry."

The guy smiled. "Really?"

"Yep. Nick is the world's best matchmaker. He'll get you hooked up in no time flat."

Jerry's face fell again. "Oh."

I said, "Come on, Jerry. It's Mardi Gras! There's tons of eligible guys around."

He frowned. "I guess."

"So what do you go for?"

He suddenly blushed.

I nodded. "Say no more. Do you like 'em tall or short?"

"About my height. Just an ordinary guy."

I nodded. "An ordinary guy who wants to fuck you, right?"

Jerry blushed again. He looked around, as if anyone could hear him, and asked, "How do you know that?"

I shrugged. "I just know. It's like magic." I thought for a moment. "So an ordinary guy. What kind of work are you in?"

He hesitated and I suddenly knew. He was in the military.

I said, "Never mind. I know."

"You do? How?"

"You're in the Navy. Are you a commander or a captain?"

He blushed again. "Uh, a commander."

Carter asked, "Did you go to Vietnam?"

Jerry nodded. "I don't get how you know all this."

I shrugged. "I'm about 20 years older than you and I've made a lotta matches."

"You're 55?"

I shrugged. "53."

"You don't look that old."

I snorted. "Thanks, Jerry."

His eyes lit up suddenly. "Oh! I love this song!"

I listened. It was new song called "Never Can Say Goodbye" by Gloria Gaynor. I looked at Jerry. "You're a romantic type, then, right?"

He nodded. "Yeah."

"So you don't really like hook-ups then, do you?"

He shook his head. "Not really. I kinda want the whole package, you know? House in the hills. White picket fence. 2.5 dogs."

I laughed. "Sounds good. How long before you retire?"

"1977 is the first year I can cash in."

I nodded and began to scan the crowd. I had no idea who I was looking for. After a moment, my attention was drawn to a man standing across Bourbon Street on the corner by the Clover Grille. He was wearing a lot of beads and his shirt was halfway open. There was something about the way he was standing that made me realize he was horny but hesitant. I'd seen that look before. "Jerry?" I said, feeling like I didn't want to spook him.

"I see him," whispered Carter in my ear. "Beads, open shirt, thumb hooked into his jeans belt loop."

I nodded.

Jerry looked up at me. "What's going on?"

Carter whispered to me. "Lemme go get him." He opened his arm and began to move away.

I put my hand on Jerry's shoulder as Carter begin to plow his way across the street. "We found someone. Carter's gone to get him."

Jerry made a face. "Are you for real?"

I nodded. "Yeah. I believe in love. And I believe in love at first sight. Carter and I are proof of that." I looked up and could see Carter leaning down to talk to the guy. "When do you have to report back to your duty station?"

"Oh eight hundred on Friday. Why?"

"When's your flight out of here?"

"I'm on space-a out of the Naval Air Station on Thursday morning."

I nodded. "Do you live alone?"

He nodded. "Yeah. I own a house in La Jolla."

"Good." I could see Carter pushing the guy through the crowd and across the street. I was about to say something to Jerry when I felt someone slap me again out of nowhere. That time, the person hit me so hard that all I could see were stars.

I heard Jerry say, "Nick? You OK?"

Nodding, I said, "I guess." Using my tongue, I checked to see if I had lost a tooth. I tasted a little blood, but nothing worse than that. "Did you see—"

Before I could finish, I heard a scuffle, and someone began yelling. The stars were finally gone, so I looked out at the curb. Carter had pinned back the arms of a man who was wearing a green and pink costume and had a mask on. The guy from across the street ripped off the mask and revealed a face I thought looked familiar, but I wasn't sure who it was.

Carter pushed the man over to where Jerry and I were standing. The man glared at me. "How dare you, sir? I ask again, how dare you?" His accent was thick, but slurred. He was obviously drunk. He had thick white hair and his face looked unnaturally smooth.

Carter pushed him forward and said, "Nick Williams, meet Reggie Jackson, our host from last night."

I nodded and suddenly understood what Miss Wanna had been talking about that morning. The memories from the night before came flooding in. I did call Mr. Jackson by that name and had said it several times during the night. I thought I was just saying his name. It never occurred to me that he, or anyone, would be insulted by it.

Jackson spit at me, hitting me in the face with it. I wiped off the spittle with the back of my hand. "What's wrong with you?"

"Niggers! Everywhere in this town! And you have the audacity to call me by that name!"

I looked up at Carter, who looked more amused than anything else.

The man from across the street, however, was definitely not amused. He got up in Jackson's face and said, "Mister, I don't know who the hell you are, but you better apologize to Mr. Williams right now. Otherwise, I'm taking you in for assault. You hear me?"

I started laughing. Jerry, Carter, Mr. Jackson, and the man from across the street all stared. I shook my head. "A cop! Of course you're a cop!" Several people walking around us suddenly stepped back and gave us a wide berth, as if I'd just announced he had the plague. I looked up at Carter. "Isn't that what Mike always says? I always find the gay cops wherever I go."

Jerry looked over at the man and asked, "Are you really a cop?"

The man nodded and grinned. "I am at that." He stuck out his hand. "My name's Bill. I hear you're a Navy man. I did time in the Corps in the Mekong Delta back in '66 and '67. And I think you're cute as a button."

Mr. Jackson struggled in Carter's arms. "What the hell is goin' on here?! Homosexual policemen? And in the Marines and the Navy? What's this city coming to?!"

Carter said, "It's called gay liberation, old man. Get used to it."

. . .

"Are you proud of yourself?" That was Carter. It was just past 11. We were both in bed, stretched out, as the party outside roared on. I had my head on his chest. Bill and Jerry were downstairs, nuzzling on the sofa the last I'd seen. We'd invited them to stay the night and to join us for breakfast the next morning at the Clover Grille. They'd agreed. Jerry had promised to be quiet. Bill had just grinned and shook his head.

"Yeah. Are you?" I ran my hand though his chest hair.

"I guess I am."

"What a day this has been. One big Fat Tuesday."

"Wanna come back next year?" asked Carter.

I sighed. "Maybe."

"Yeah, me neither."

I laughed. "It was fun. But I don't think I'm cut out for this much fun all at one time."

"We're too old."

I sat up and looked down at him. "Speak for yourself. You heard Jerry. I can't possibly be 53."

Carter lifted his arm up and ran his hand through my hair. "You'll always be 24. You'll always be the man I saw walk through the door, across a crowded room."

I leaned down and kissed him on the lips. "And you'll always be 26. You'll be the big hunk of a fireman I saw leaning against the bar, looking like the most handsome man in North America." I kissed him again. "Or that's all I knew back then. Now I know you're the most handsome man on six continents. We've still never been to Antarctica, so we have some more exploring to do."

He kissed me back. "We've come a long way, baby."

I stretched out next to him and said, "We sure have."

St. David's Day
1848

Preface

This story, as you might have noticed from the title, is not in the scope of time as the other stories.

That is because this tale doesn't take place in time at all, except for the brief moments where we find Griffith Williams and where we leave him.

Enjoy!

The Story

Along the River Taff
Rhydyfelin, Wales
Wednesday, March 1, 1848
Early morning

    Nick walked aboard the boat tied up alongside the rickety dock and, ducking his head, made his way through the door and inside the cabin. He knew it was chilly inside. However, in the small kitchen on the forward end of the boat, he could see a bit of light coming from the stove. He figured there was some coal inside, doing its best to keep the place warm
    In the dark, the interior looked older than he remembered from when he'd visited in his dreams. There was more junk, for one thing, and he had the sense that a kind of dank smell permeated the place.
    That made him think of Carter which, for whatever reason, seemed to light up the room for a brief moment.

Smiling to himself, Nick turned and went into the aft part of the boat and found a narrow bed there, pushed to one side. It was covered with a thick pile of wool blankets, none of which were very clean.

Under the heavy covers, he saw the blond head of the man he knew to be Gwyn Owen, his great-grandfather's close friend and lover. Gwyn was snoring, his head bent back a little and his thin nose pointing straight up. A little ball of spit was resting in the corner of the man's mouth.

Just tucked under his chin was the dark and tousled head of Griffith Williams, Nick's great-grandfather.

Neither man was clean, to say the least, and Nick knew the room smelled to high heaven. He was glad Carter hadn't come with him. If he had, his ethereal nose would have been twitching in disgust. Thinking of Carter made the room light up, again.

Gwyn frowned in his sleep and turned on his side.

Griffy (that was the nickname Gwyn had used when Nick had met them in his dreams) shifted as well. Doing so made the covers slip off his face. Reaching up from under, he used a grimy finger to scratch his nose.

"Great-grandfather?"

Griffy sighed to himself but didn't open his eyes.

"Great-grandfather?"

Taking a deep breath and then coughing, Griffy shifted in the bed again. That movement made Gwyn mutter to himself. Nick had no idea what the man was saying. He couldn't tell if it was Welsh or just the sounds that a deep sleeper made when he was disturbed.

"Griffy?" asked Nick.

"What be?" muttered his great-grandfather, his eyes still closed.

"Wake up."

Finally, the man's eyes opened. He took one look at

the Nick's ghostly form standing by his bed and frowned.

...

Griffy was certain he was dreaming.

Why else would he be seeing a man in such strange clothes and with eyes the color of brown ale?

To be certain, he was a handsome one, he was. Griffy felt the warmth which told him a roll around might be a good morning spent.

But there was something familiar in the face. Who did it remind him of, he wondered?

Then, like that, he knew.

And any warmth faded away, as fast as it had come.

"Why be you here?"

"What?"

"Why do you disturb my rest?"

"I'm here to take you to lunch."

"Go back to the place you belong." He wasn't afraid of any spirit, but he had no desire to spend time with the man he hated and despised and whom he'd buried five years past, come the fifth of April.

The man laughed. When he did, Griffy began to doubt—

Sitting up, sudden-like, Griffy asked, "Who be you? In truth."

"I'm your great-grandson, Nicholas."

What sort of answer was that? A great-grandfather? At his age and not yet married nor any prospects to be?

Griffy snorted. "What you might be, demon from Hell or spirit from Heaven, I cannot say. But a great-grandfather or father of any kind, I am not." He waved the apparition away. "Now, be off and let me rest."

Then came that smile again. "But they're waiting for you."

"Who's waitin'?"

"Everyone. We're having leek and potato soup. It's St. David's Day, after all."

Griffy nodded and, realizing his hunger, asked, "And where will we eat? Have you brought the *cawl cennin* with you?"

"What's that?"

Laughing, Griffy said, "Leek soup with potato and cream, if you're of a mind to add it and have some ready t'hand." He winked. "And you say you're a Welshman, do you?"

The man shook his head. "I'm an American."

"That explains your speech, then."

"Sure."

"Where from in America? New York?"

"San Francisco."

"Never heard of it."

The man smiled. "It's in California."

"That so? I read about a war there between America and Mexico, I think it was."

"Oh, right. I guess—"

Griffy was in no mind to discuss news from far away. He was tired. "Go on about your way, spirit, and leave me to my rest."

Shaking his head, the man replied, "Sorry, Griffy, no can do. We're going to be late for lunch."

Griffy snorted and pulled the blankets over his head, hoping the spirit would leave him be.

. . .

"Come on," said Nick.

"No," was the reply under the covers.

Nick was stumped. He knew that his great-grandfather had to get out bed of his own free will. That was the only way for him to go to where they were going. He thought for a long moment and then had an idea.

"How would you like to see the future?"

"What future?"

"How things turn out for you."

"Be they good or be they ill, I'll have my rest, thank you."

"Why do you sound like Shakespeare sometimes?"

No answer.

"Well?" asked Nick.

Moving the covers off his face, his great-grandfather looked at Nick for a moment before asking, "What do you know of the Bard?"

Nick shrugged. "I've read some of his plays."

"And the sonnets?"

"In high school."

"*Mine be thy love and thy love's use their treasure.*"

"What's that?"

"The final line of one of the sonnets, it is."

Nick shrugged.

"T'is speakin' of the love of a man for a man." Griffy stared at Nick intently.

"Would you like to meet my husband?"

Obviously surprised, Griffy asked, "*Husband*?"

"Carter Jones. He's a fireman. In San Francisco. Or, at least, he was."

"Jones?" asked Griffy with a twinkle in his eye. "A true Welshman, I'd wager."

Nick nodded. "Yeah."

"From where?"

"Georgia. In America."

Griffy rolled his eyes. "Another one who's left us, has he?"

"His ancestors did."

Griffy stared at him.

Nick asked, "Would you like to meet him?"

"Your *husband*?"

"Yeah."

"Does that make you the wife?" asked Griffy with a leer.

"We're both husbands."

Glancing over at Gwyn, who was still sound asleep, Griffy said, "That can't be so. There's a wife and there's a husband."

"What about Gwyn?"

His great-grandfather's eyes widened a bit. "How do you know his name?"

Nick wasn't sure how to answer that question, so he didn't. He just stared at Griffy.

"Why do you look at me like this?"

"Like what?"

"As if you see me to my bones."

Nick shrugged. "All I want is for you to get out of bed and follow me." He added, "It'll be warmer where we're going," and immediately wished he hadn't.

Griffy immediately slid down further in the bed and yanked the covers over his head. "Be gone, foul demon."

Nick couldn't help but laugh. "You sound like Shakespeare again."

After a few seconds, Griffy said, "Is that so?"

"Yeah."

"Are you a demon or have you come to take me to heaven?"

"Neither."

Still under the covers, Griffy sighed. "Who be you?"

"Your great-grandson."

"I've no living kin."

"Not yet."

Griffy sat up a little and peered over the edge of the sheet. "Not yet?"

"Once you move—" Nick stopped, not sure if he should say more. Not until his Uncle Paul was around, at least.

"Move? Move where?"

"San Francisco."

"Mexico?"

"America."

Griffy sat up a bit more and pushed the covers down a little. "Why?"

"That's why I'm here and that's what lunch is about. Don't you want to get out of bed and follow me?" Nick wasn't impatient. Not like he used to be. But he missed Carter, and—

Griffy winced as the room got bright like it had before. "What is that light?"

Nick smiled. "I was thinking of my husband and—"

It happened again.

For some reason, that made Griffy laugh. "Tell me about him, this husband of yours."

Nick smiled as the room lit up and stayed lit. "He's tall and just about the most handsome man you'll ever meet. When he's building a fire, his back is big and broad and—"

Griffy put his arm over his face. "Now, now. That's enough of that. You're fairly blindin' me, you are."

Nick laughed. "Sorry, Griffy."

All of a sudden, his great-grandfather pushed back the covers, revealing the fact that the only thing he wore to bed was a strange pair of yellowed BVDs and some thin black wool socks. He jumped up and then pulled a kind of dressing gown off the back of an old chair. "You say it will be warm, do you?"

Nick nodded. "We're having lunch in the garden."

"Is it a palace where you live?" Griffy was buttoning up his gown, if that's what it was called.

"Nope. Just a big pile of rocks."

"Rocks?"

Nick laughed. "That's a joke. It's the house your oldest son, Michael, built."

Griffy stopped what he was doing. "No son of mine will ever be called Michael."

Nick shrugged. "What about your wife? Won't she have a say in things like that?"

Griffy snorted. "I suppose..."

Nick turned and began to make his way towards the door that led outside.

"Where might you be off to, spirit?"

"San Francisco."

"I might as well follow you, I suppose."

They were out on the rickety dock, by then. Nick laughed to himself and, mostly under his breath, said, "*Be sure to wear some flowers in your hair.*"

"Is that poetry?" asked his great-grandfather as the night air around them began to fade.

"No, it's hippie talk."

"Hippie? What might that be?"

...

Paul Williams stepped out into the garden of his brother's house and smiled. His great-niece, Janet, was sitting on a bench, basking in the sun, and holding hands with her beloved, Lenora. The two women made a perfect pair.

Lenora reminded him of a darker, plumper Josephine Baker, a singer he'd not seen perform in Paris (her arrival there coincided with his years in the Orient), but whom he'd met shortly before his own demise (such a quaint word).

Paul was content with his arrangements to see his father after so long. In the afterlife, impatience was no longer quite the force it had been when he was in corporeal form. However, he still had a strong sense that time was running out, somehow, and that it was time to inform his father of his destiny.

Paul stood in the doorway and watched as the two girls cooed and whispered, each kissing the other and obviously enjoying their time in the sun.

Time. *Time.*

But what was time on this side of the veil? Time never passed. Not for him. True, he could watch it passing for the living. But, for the dead, they lived in an eternal now which did change, but the changes were never marked by time.

"Uncle Paul?"

Turning, he looked up into the bright emerald green eyes of Carter Jones, the beloved of his dear great-nephew, Nicholas. "Yes, my boy?"

"Shouldn't they be here by now?"

"They are getting closer. My father was always a stubborn old fool. I feel quite certain that, in his youth, he was just as stubborn, if not as foolish."

Carter smiled in reply to that.

. . .

"You said t'weren't a palace."

Nick looked over at his great-grandfather. They were standing in front of the house on Sacramento Street. Instead of wearing the odd dressing gown he'd put on just a few moments ago, Griffy was decked out in a more formal affair. It was a dark brown checkered suit with a high collar and a matching tie. Nick was sure he'd seen a photograph of his great-grandfather dressed just like that somewhere before.

"It isn't," he replied. Turning to his left, he pointed to the big Crocker Mansion, a towering gothic masterpiece covered in gingerbread, and said, "Now, that's a palace."

"Yes, t'is." replied Griffy with the sound of awe in his voice.

. . .

"Now this is a fireplace where I can warm my bones," said Griffy as he stood in front of the fire, stretching out his hands to feel the heat.

"Carter makes the best fires."

"What is the name of his vessel?"

"His vessel?"

Griffy turned to look at the spirit, who was glowing once again. "You say he's a fireman. Does he work on one of the big steamships?"

The spirit laughed, his brown eyes twinkling in the light. "No, he doesn't stoke fires, he puts out fires."

"Now, why would he do that?"

"To protect things like homes and other buildings here in the City."

"Ah," replied Griffy. "Well, whatever he may do, if he built this fire, I want to shake his hand, I do."

"Here he is," replied the spirit.

Griffy couldn't help but smile as a handsome green-eyed giant loomed over him. Being a courteous man, he said, "I thank you for the warmth of this fire."

"You're welcome. It's nice to finally meet you."

"That so?"

The giant shifted where he stood and, in a voice weaker than it should have been, said, "Your son, Paul, wants to talk to you."

Laughing at the fire, Griffy said, "I have no wife and have done nothing which would bring forth a son."

"More Shakespeare," muttered the spirit.

The giant frowned. "He's just outside in the garden, Mr. Williams."

"Mister, is it?"

"Yes, sir."

"*Sir?*"

The giant looked at the spirit. "Uh, Nick? Help?"

The spirit shrugged.

"Griffith?" asked the giant.

"Yes?"

"Would you like to come outside with us?"

"Is it warmer there than by this fire?"

Both nodded with vigor. "Definitely," replied the giant.

"Then, let us go."

"Sheesh," said the spirit, as if to the wind.

. . .

Standing next to Janet and Lenora, Paul was delighted to witness his father step out from inside the house and emerge into the garden, followed, as he was, by both Nicholas and Carter.

Stepping forward, Paul extended a hand in friendship and affection. "Father."

The man stopped. He appeared to be confused. "I am no man's father."

Nicholas sighed, somewhat impatiently. In a fit of pique, he said, "Yeah, yeah, we know that. You're a goddam Kinsey 6."

With a wink, Carter offered a patient grin. Putting his large hands on Griffith's shoulder, he said, "This is Paul. He'll be your second son when he's born."

"That so?" asked the man, sounding more Welsh and less English than he had a moment earlier.

Paul nodded. He took one further step forward and took his father's hand in his own. "Yes, Father. Michael will arrive first. I won't be too far behind."

"Michael?" asked the man with a scowl. "What manner of name is that for a Welshman?"

Paul knew the answer. Their mother had wanted her children to bear her uncles' names. Paul also knew it was a point of contention for his parents. Instead of trudging down that garden path, he said, "Michael built this house."

Looking around with interest, his father said, "T'ain't bad."

Knowing full well that was high praise, Paul replied, "It will last for generations, Father."

With an exasperated sigh, Griffith looked his son in the eye and said, "So, are you all spirits? Have you summoned me to this place to tempt me to some one thing or t'other?"

. . .

Nick couldn't remember the last time he'd felt so annoyed at anyone or anything. Being dead had its perks. Not feeling frustrated by much of anything was definitely one of them.

But his great-grandfather was beginning to rub him the wrong way. He could feel himself getting worked up as if it was '51 or '52 and he was trying to collect on a deadbeat loan.

He stepped around and put his hands on his hips. "Look, we're here to give you some great news. It would help if you'd be a little less stubborn and a little more grateful." Looking up at the warm sun in the sky, he added, "When was the last time you were this warm?"

The look he got in reply was a flash of anger coupled with some amusement. "If I be your sire, indeed, *bach*, then why do you speak this way to me? Have you no respect?"

Nick couldn't help but grin. He leaned forward and kissed the man on the cheek.

It had the effect he'd been hoping for. Griffy put his hand on his face and looked astonished. "What's this, *bach*?"

"What does that mean, Nick?" asked Janet as she walked towards the two of them.

He looked at her and replied, "I think it's a Welsh term of affection."

"T'is," replied Griffy with a wink. "And it's a reminder that, though we may look the same age, I am the elder and you'd be good to remember the same." He grinned at Janet. "I see my mother's face in yours. Would you be my great-granddaughter, then?"

She smiled. "Yes, sir."

"*Sir?*" asked Griffy. But, instead of sounding insulted like he had with Carter, he laughed and patted her cheek affectionately.

. . .

"Now, then," said Griffy, sitting in his proper place at the head of the table. He pushed back his bowl of soup, he asked, "Apart from this *cawl*, which is as good as any I've ever tasted, why have you summoned me from my rest?"

"Apart from the sunshine and the warm fire?" asked the girl, Janet, with a defiant tone not unlike his mother's.

"Am I the head of this family?" demanded Griffy.

"Yes," replied his kin as the others looked on.

"Well, then, the questions I'll be asking and not you, *bach*." He winked at the girl to set her at ease.

"Uncle Paul has something he needs to tell you," said Nicholas.

"And?"

"Something of momentous import is about to happen, Father."

"That so?"

"Yes." The boy, who was as fancy as any toff Griffy had ever spied near or around Cardiff Castle, spoke in measured tones. "Not far from here, some men have discovered gold. And, before long, you'll read about it in the newspaper."

"Will I, now?"

"Yes. It won't be an easy journey, but it is important that you depart from Wales and come to live here."

"And why might that be?"

"You'll make your fortune here, Father."

"And why not in Wales? There's money to be made everywhere you look."

Nicholas, who appeared to be as impatient as a hungry hen, spoke out of turn. "If you don't come to California, you won't meet your wife and none of us will ever be born."

Griffy felt the weight of those words without knowing why. He looked around the table. The dark girl next to his Janet smiled at him and said, "It won't hurt me none, Mr. Williams." She then took Janet's hand in hers and added, "But then I won't meet the love of my life and I can't imagine you'd begrudge me that joy."

He liked the sound of her speech. Smiling, he leaned forward a bit, and asked, "And where are you from, my girl?"

"Alabama."

"Is that in America?"

"Yes, s—" She put her hand over her mouth and then laughed. "Yes, it is."

"What be your name?"

"Lenora."

He winked at her and turned to Carter, the giant. "Georgia?"

"Yes." He smiled at Lenora. "It's the next state over from Alabama."

"I see," replied Griffy. He scratched his chin thoughtfully. "Will you not be born should I not sail to California?"

"No." He frowned. "But I can't imagine my life without Nick."

Turning to Paul, Griffy asked, "And where is your beloved, my son?"

"I had many loves in my lifetime, Father, but none of them were my true beloved."

Not knowing why, Griffy felt a tear come to his eye. Wiping it away, he was surprised to hear himself say, "T'is a fate we share, *bach*."

Paul nodded with a serious face. "Yes, Father. I think it is."

. . .

Nick sighed with relief. Griffy was finally beginning to understand why he was there and how important it was for him to go to California.

"Why should I wait to sail?"

Nick thought that was a good question.

Uncle Paul had an answer. "Your friend, Gwyn Owen, should travel with you. He won't be ready as soon as you are."

"You know about him, do you?"

"Now, I do. You never told us about him during your lifetime."

Blushing a little, Griffy said, "T'is no wonder, if what you say is true. Wouldn't be right for a proper man with a wife and two sons to speak of such things."

Nick got a quick glimpse of the man he knew his great-grandfather would become. It was a shame, really. The man at the head of the table was happy and light-hearted. He wouldn't always be like that. Nick had seen as much in his dreams when he was alive.

But, then again, if Griffy hadn't become a tyrant once he was older and had more money, Uncle Paul would never have taken off and traveled to Paris and Shanghai and everywhere else he went. That was part of the reason he'd made all the money he did. In the end, Uncle Paul had died many times wealthier than his father.

Janet was obviously thinking along the same lines. She piped up and said, "But, don't forget how you are now, great-grandfather. That'll be important when you get older."

"Will it now, *bach*?" He winked at her. "Well, then, I'll endeavor to do just that." He looked at Uncle Paul. "Now, you say my fortune is to be made in California..."

"Yes, Father."

"How will I do that, if I may ask?"

"Being a miner," said Uncle Paul, "you will know more than most how to find and extract the gold when you get here."

Griffy nodded. He thought for a moment and then frowned. "But what of the expense for the passage? I've set aside close to ten pound, but I doubt that will carry me across the Atlantic and around Cape Horn."

Uncle Paul smiled. "We can't tell you everything, Father, but keep an eye open for news of the death of the Marquess of Bute." Nick knew that was the man who pretty much ran things in and around Cardiff.

Looking surprised, Griffy said, "That toff?"

"Yes, Father. He's about to die and, well..." He glanced over at Carter. "Something to your advantage will happen as a result."

"Well," was all that Griffy had to say about that. A couple of beats later, he yawned into the back of his hand.

Nick stood and walked over to the head of the table. "Come on. Time to get you back to bed."

Without making a fuss, the man stood. He then looked around the table as everyone else followed his lead. "What a night it's been."

And, just like that, the room began to fade away and everyone with it.

. . .

Griffy stretched and yawned. The day was breaking just outside, and the morning was cold.

"Some dreams you had," whispered Gwyn in his ear.

"Dreams?"

"You turned and tossed and talked and talked. I tried to wake you, but you were determined to stay sleeping."

Griffy turned, pulled Gwyn's head close, and kissed his forehead. "What dreams? I slept like a babe."

"As I said, you talked and talked."

"And what about?"

"About California and gold and you spoke out names—Nicholas, Paul, Janet. There was more, but I didn't understand much of any of it."

A hazy idea of something or another passed through Griffy's mind, but he couldn't make it make sense. Instead, he murmured, "Did I, now?" and dove under the warm blankets to start St. David's Day right with Gwyn.

. . .

To his delight, Nick found himself walking along the beach, hand in hand with the man he loved forever.

Carter said, "You did good, son."

"Thanks. He was stubborn, but I think we got through to him."

"We must have." He leaned around and kissed Nick on the lips. "After all, you're still here."

"Did you think I would vanish?"

"I wasn't worried."

"Me neither."

They walked along in silence for a long while before coming to a spot in the sand where Carter pulled Nick down and began to make love to him, just like he always had and always would.

Even in the afterlife.

Author's Note

Thank you for buying and reading this story!

This story, like all the others I've written, came to me out of thin air.

Many thanks, as always, to everyone who has read, reviewed, and emailed me about all of my books. It is deeply gratifying in ways that words will never be able to fully express. Thank you.

. . .

For news about upcoming books, subscribe to my newsletter here:

http://frankwbutterfield.com/subscribe

About
Frank W. Butterfield

Although Frank worships San Francisco, he lives at the beach on another coast. Born on a windy day in November of 1966, he was elected President of his high school Spanish Club in the spring of 1983. After moving across these United States like a rapid-fire pinball, he now makes his home in a hurricane-proof motel, built in 1947, with superior water pressure. While he hasn't met any dolphins personally, that invitation is always open.

. . .

Frank W. Butterfield is the Amazon best-selling author of 59 (and counting) self-published novels, novellas, and short stories.

Born in Lubbock, Texas, Frank grew up there, in the Dallas area, and under the pine and cypress surrounding Caddo Lake.

A Westerner, he graduated from Lubbock High School in 1984. He was fortunate to be an exchange student in La Serena, Chile, in the second half of 1982. He attended the University of Texas in Austin and, after three semesters, realized he was wasting his time and his parents' money and dropped out.

Moving to New York City in 1987, Frank worked in the hospitality industry for several years while also moving from there to San Francisco and to Provincetown before returning to Texas in 1992.

Making Austin his home a second time, he finally settled into a corporate job and taught himself to write code and manage projects in Austin and Washington, D.C. After ten years of being what he likes to call "a normal person" he left the security of making a living in a "real job" and decided to strike out on his own.

Spending several years traveling around the U.S. and Canada, he found himself drawn to Daytona Beach, Florida, where he now resides.

His initial novel, *The Unexpected Heiress*, was self-published on June 1, 2016. 59 books later, the stories keep coming, right out of thin air!

Credits

Yesteryear Font (headings) used with permission under SIL Open Font License, Version 1.1. Copyright © 2011 by Brian J. Bonislawsky DBA Astigmatic (AOETI). All rights reserved.

Gentium Book Basic Font (body text) used with permission under the SIL Open Font License, Version 1.1. Copyright © 2002 by J. Victor Gaultney. All rights reserved.

FOGLIHTENNO07 Font (cover text) used with permission under the SIL Open Font License, Version 1.1. Copyright © 2011-2015 by gluk (www.glukfonts.pl | gluksza@wp.pl). All rights reserved.

Cover image of St. David's Cathedral, Pembrokeshire, Wales, licensed under copyright from Lenise Calleja / 123RF Stock Photo. Original imege edited to make it appear older.

New Year's sketch licensed under copyright from Anton Kubalík / 123RF Stock Photo.

MLK sketch licensed under copyright from olenaboldyreva / 123RF Stock Photo.

Cherub sketch licensed under copyright from sea-martini / 123RF Stock Photo.

Washington sketch licensed under copyright from Chen Yunpeng / 123RF Stock Photo.

Mardi Gras mask sketch licensed under copyright from jemastock / 123RF Stock Photo.

Welsh flag and icon sketches licensed under copyright from Anna Kniazeva / 123RF Stock Photo.

More Information

Be the first to know about new releases:

frankwbutterfield.com

Made in the USA
Columbia, SC
13 March 2020